BLUE PLATE SPECIAL

BLUE PLATE SPECIAL

•

Cheri Jetton

AVALON BOOKS
NEW YORK

PRINTED IN THE UNITED STATES OF AMERICA
ON ACID-FREE PAPER
BY HADDON CRAFTSMEN, BLOOMSBURG, PENNSYLVANIA

I dedicate this, my first published novel, to the memory of my husband, John. You always told me I could do it, darling, and I have the memory of your unwavering support to thank for this accomplishment. I love you.

Chapter One

Megan held her breath and prayed, *just a little further, you can do it, don't give out yet.* The car ignored her pleas. The engine missed again, then died altogether. She slapped the steering wheel in frustration and guided the disabled vehicle to the side of the divided highway. *Darn!* What would she do now?

If she could make it to Houston, she'd surely find a job there. She'd driven from Kansas City across most of Texas. With less than twenty dollars in her purse and about three hundred available on her lone credit card, she couldn't afford any more automotive repairs. A blown tire in McAlester, Oklahoma, and a ruptured water hose outside of Ennis, Texas, had cut into her funds severely.

Who was she kidding? Even if she abandoned the

car and took a bus from here, she didn't have enough for more than a few days' food and lodging.

The car rolled to a stop and she set the parking brake. "I don't even know where *here* is," she grumbled to herself as she climbed out. She raised the hood and gave the engine compartment a cursory inspection. The fan belt looked fine and nothing appeared to be leaking or spouting steam—or flames. She dusted her hands and stepped back, having exhausted the limits of her trouble-shooting abilities.

The mechanic in Ennis had checked the oil and re-filled the water after replacing the hose, and she'd re-fueled then as well, so it couldn't be anything like that.

A pickup-truck pulling a horse trailer sped by, buffeting her with a blast of hot air and a shower of grit. She pushed the fly-away strands of honey blond hair back from her face and swiped at the trickle of perspiration that tracked down from her temple.

"Well, old girl," she told the battered little Ford, "I guess this is it. You gave it your best shot and that's all anyone can expect." She gently patted the fender. "I'll miss you."

The next logical step would be to figure out where in the Sam Hill she was, so Megan retrieved her road map and spread it on the car's roof. Tall stands of pine and undergrowth pushed up against the fence line edging the highway right of way, but cast no shade up on the graveled verge. Hot, glaring rays from the sun bounced off the car's surface. Another salty trickle ran down the back of her neck.

Pinning the map in place with one hand, she traced her route with a forefinger, but before she could pinpoint her location, she heard the crunch of tires followed by the slam of a car door. A masculine voice called out at the same time, "Need some help, ma'am?"

A lanky, dark-haired cowboy approached from the oldest, boxiest pickup truck she'd ever seen. It had to be a 1950s vintage at the latest. Overall, with its faded red paint, the truck looked to be in worse shape than her Ford Escort. *At least his truck is running.* "More than you can guess," she said under her breath as he stopped next to her.

"Ma'am?"

She swung her attention from the pickup to its driver. Deep blue eyes gazed down at her from the shadow of a summer straw western hat.

"I said, yes," she amended. "Yes, I do."

"Would you like me to look at the car for you?"

"Look all you'd like, but I don't think it's going to help." She sighed. "Too many miles, too much neglect. Takes its toll on the best of us, I'm afraid."

The man nodded and touched the brim of his hat in silent salute, then stepped around her and strode to the front of the car. His boot heels crunched in the gravel and kicked up little eddies of dust.

A van sped by, scouring them with more dust and heat. The man thumbed his hat back from his forehead and braced his hands on the fender. "What was it doing before it stopped?" he asked in a low soft drawl as he bent his tall frame to peer under the hood.

"It was going," Megan muttered.

The cowboy straightened slowly, propped his hands on lean hips, and fixed her with a cool stare. "No spit?" he questioned, his voice heavy with sarcasm.

Immediately ashamed of herself, she dropped her gaze. He *was* trying to help; she had no reason to smart off. She glanced up again. "I'm sorry. This day has just been one disaster after another."

She offered an apologetic smile. He nodded his acceptance and gestured to the engine with a nod of his head. "Try to start it."

Megan knew it wouldn't do any good, but she obeyed. "Seems to be electrical," he called from under the hood. "Turn the key off."

He wiggled the battery connections, then went to his truck for tools. After scraping the corrosion from around the battery terminals, he tightened the cables and had her try it again. Still nothing.

"If it's any help," she called, "the red light with the picture of a battery came on about an hour before the engine died."

His head appeared from around the hood and a slow, sexy grin climbed one side of his tanned face. "Yes, ma'am, that is a help. Sounds like the voltage regulator went out."

"Oh." She sighed and slumped in her seat. "Well, that's that then."

The cowboy shut the hood and pulled a bandana

from his hip pocket. He wiped his hands and offered, "I'll give you a ride into Huntsville, then see what I can do about getting it running again."

Megan studied him from the relative safety of her car's interior. He looked okay; friendly expression, relaxed stance, and he certainly seemed polite enough, but a person just couldn't be too careful these days.

When she didn't answer, a warm smile eased over his features, crinkling his eyes at the corners. "Accepting a ride from a stranger might make you a little uneasy, but I don't want to leave you out in this heat." He again reached for his hip pocket. "I have identification, and I'll even let you hold onto my wallet until we get there."

That smile alone tempted Megan to abandon good judgment, but just then a Texas Highway Patrol cruiser pulled off the road in front of her car. "Problems, Chad?" the trooper called as he climbed out and settled his cream-colored Stetson hat into place.

The cowboy grinned and replied, "A couple. The first is mechanical, but you might be able to lend a hand with the second."

"Sure thing." The officer approached. "What can I do?"

The man named Chad nodded to her. "I need a character reference. Don't want to leave the lady out in this heat while I see to her car, but she's nervous about accepting rides with strangers."

"Wise woman."

Chad smiled down at her. "True."

"Tell you what, why don't I give her a ride? You taking her to The Depot?"

"Yeah, but I wouldn't want to put you out any."

Megan saw a sparkle of mischief in the officer's eyes when he replied, "It's no trouble, Chad, no trouble at all. In fact, rescuing ladies in distress is what I do best."

Chad leaned a forearm on the roof of her little vehicle. "Well, miss, looks like your problem's solved. This nice policeman here will get you safely out of the sun."

The crackle of the patrol car's radio diverted everyone's attention. After answering the call, the trooper reported, "We'll need to make it quick. A truck just tried taking that exit ramp south of town too fast and rolled on its side."

Megan glanced from Chad to the officer and back. The state trooper was obviously acquainted with her Samaritan. He also knew the cowboy would be giving her a ride. "Thanks, but that's okay, you go ahead." She smiled and nodded at Chad. "You've more or less vouched for his character, I'll ride with him."

The patrolman sighed dramatically. "Oh well, win some and lose some."

"But thank you for the offer," she quickly added.

He grinned and touched the brim of his hat. "Any time, ma'am. You take care now. See you 'round, Chad."

The cowboy pushed away from her car and Megan climbed out. While he retrieved his tools and put them away, she began unloading her suitcases. She'd lugged the largest one to the side of his truck then returned to grasp two smaller cases, when he noticed.

"What're you doing?"

"You said I could ride to Huntsville with you," she replied, tugging at the bags.

"You can leave your things in the car, I'll be back for it."

"It's dead. You said so." She staggered back a step as the second bag popped loose. He steadied her with a hand at her spine and took the luggage from her hand.

"It can be fixed."

"I've already poured more into it on this trip than it's worth. I can't afford to throw good money after bad."

He looked exasperated, but his tone was the slow, patient one used to explain things to small children. "You can get a rebuilt regulator for about fifty dollars."

"Fifty dollars? That would get me a place to sleep and a meal," she shot back, "plus I'd have to pay a mechanic a lot more than that to put it on."

"I'd put it on for you, it doesn't take a mechanic to do it."

Megan reached into her car again, then paused in the unloading. "Look, that's awfully nice of you, but it's just more than I can afford to part with right now."

Chad studied her for a moment, then shook his

head. "Okay, let's get this stuff in the truck. Where're you headed?"

"Huntsville."

"I mean in the long run." He tucked another of the small bags under his arm. "Maybe I can get you a ride."

"Thanks, but Huntsville will do for now," she told his retreating back.

The sun beat down mercilessly and she wondered if south Texas was always this hot in September. It had to be at least ninety-five degrees out here. She swiped her forearm across her brow before reaching into the car for a carton. A shadow fell over her as she struggled with the box.

"Do the doors lock?" Chad asked from just over her shoulder.

"Yes, but . . ."

"Then just lock it up, I'll send a wrecker for it before anyone has a chance to steal anything."

She snorted. "There's really nothing worth stealing."

"Maybe," he husked in that slow, sweet drawl, "but it's worth something to you, otherwise you wouldn't have carted it all the way from Kansas."

"How did you . . . of course, my license plates."

He grinned at her and held out a hand. "By the way, I'm Chad Winslow."

"Meg . . ." Her voice trailed off as his large hand completely engulfed hers. Warm, strong, hard. She swallowed. "Megan Stallings."

"Pleased t'meet you. Now let's get out of this sun before it boils our brains."

He returned the box to her car, locked it, then took her elbow and escorted her to his truck where he helped her in. When he'd swung himself into the driver's side and slammed the door, he tested it. It held and he flashed her a quick smile. "Can't be too careful, she's not as young as she used to be."

He turned the key and shifted into gear. "Buckle up, Miss Stallings, and we'll go find something cold to drink."

Recovering her good sense now that he was no longer touching her, Megan replied primly, "Thank you, Mr. Winslow, but if you'll just drop me at the first gas station or cafe we come to . . ."

A low chuckle rumbled from the other side of the truck. "I'm not going to make off with you, Miss Stallings, I just thought you looked like you could use a cold glass of tea . . . at the first cafe we come to, okay?"

"Okay." Megan relaxed. "Thank you, Mr. Winslow."

"Chad."

"Chad. Call me Meg."

"If you don't mind, I like Megan better." Her glance flew to his face, but he was looking over his left shoulder as he pulled onto the highway.

She found the ends of an old-fashioned set of seat belts and snapped them together, then pulled the strap to take up the slack. A road sign announced fifteen miles to Huntsville and eighty to Houston. *So near, yet so far.* The truck picked up speed and the wind from the open windows ruffled her hair and dried the perspiration from her face and neck. She sighed, closed her eyes, and let her head fall back against the bench seat. Things could be worse. Her rescuer could have had a beer gut, bad teeth, and been spitting tobacco juice. Instead, he looked like every woman's fantasy of the American cowboy.

Even with her eyes closed the man beside her filled her senses. The smell of sun-dried cotton and spicy aftershave mingled with the salty tang of honest sweat—a deliciously masculine potpourri emanating from a decidedly masculine specimen. She gave herself a small grunt of disgust and sat up straight in the seat.

"Do you live around here?" she asked.

"All my life."

"What kind of work is available?"

The man beside her chuckled. "Well, I run a cattle spread, but I don't think that's what you're looking for."

"Not quite." Megan smiled and lapsed into silence.

A few minutes later Chad pointed down the road to a large truck stop. "How's that?"

"Perfect."

They pulled in and he ushered her through the cafe door with a light touch at the small of her back. At the check-out stand he paused and kissed the slightly plump, middle-aged cashier on the cheek. "Hi, Mom."

"Hi yourself, honey. Who you got there?"

"Found me a tourist wandering around." He grinned at Megan. "This is Miss Megan Stallings from Kansas. Megan, my mother and proprietress of this fine establishment, Eileen Winslow."

His mother? "How do you do, Mrs. Winslow? My car broke down and your son was kind enough give me a lift."

A waitress dressed in incredibly tight jeans and a closely fitted sleeveless shirt approached and purred to Chad, "You can give me a lift anytime you want, darlin', you don't have to be pickin' up road kill."

Megan heard every word, although she doubted the young woman intended the comment for her ears. Was she a member of the family too, a kissing cousin perhaps? A flash of irritation drew Megan's brows into a scowl, but the next moment she tried to hide a smile. Chad was blushing a deep red and doing some scowling of his own.

"Nadine," Eileen said sweetly, "I believe you have an order up."

"Yes, ma'am, I believe I do," the girl cooed, giving Chad a lascivious smirk before moving off.

Chad glanced uneasily at Megan, then nodded to a back corner of the large room. "If you'd like to freshen up, the ladies' room is over there. I'll get us some tea."

"Thanks, I'd appreciate that."

* * *

Megan raised tired eyes to the mirror and decided *road kill* may have been too kind a description. Her face was grimy from the blowing dust and smeared where sweat had streaked the dirt. Her hair flew out in a dozen different directions, only a small portion of it still confined at her nape in a ponytail. Dark circles underscored her brown eyes.

Her hand dove into her purse, searching out the items needed to repair her appearance. *Just look at yourself, Megan Stallings! You were worried about accepting a ride from a stranger, but it took one awfully brave man to even make the offer. You look like a fugitive from . . .* Megan stopped and stared, her heart sinking to her stomach where it trembled in fear.

She'd run from the notoriety, that definitely made her a coward. Whether she was a legal fugitive or not remained to be seen. Did that mean the cowboy would be in trouble for helping her? Surely not. He knew nothing about her.

Her stomach clenched. "Snap out of it," she growled at herself, "you're just overly tired. Hysterics aren't the answer and self-pity was never your style."

A deep, cleansing breath steadied her. She loosened her hair and began brushing at the tangles. Her attention focused on the mirror as stroke after stroke she sought to tame the flyaway strands. She pushed all negative thoughts to the back of her mind.

Her hair once again smooth and fastened back, she bent over the basin to wash her face. Handfuls of water cooled her parched skin and the liquid hand soap loosened the grime. She rinsed, then patted her face dry. That had been refreshing. *Almost as refreshing as the look in that cowboy's eyes.*

"Back off," she muttered to the little voice. "So he gives your pulse a kick-start, it's just hormones. And that's what got you in this mess to begin with."

Chad watched her go, his hands jammed into his back pockets.

"Pretty little thing."

He looked over at his mother's innocent expression. "Yeah. Yeah, she is." His attention returned to Megan's departing figure and he cleared his throat. "Uh, Mom, I think she's kinda down on her luck. Can we help her out?"

"I don't see why not, but, Chad . . ."

"I know, I know. Don't worry about me."

"That'll be the day," his mother chuckled.

He dropped into the nearest booth and called out, "Hey, Celia, how about a couple of iced teas over here."

Yeah, she's a pretty little package all right, and all tied up with a sassy mouth. His lips quirked as he remembered her muttered, "it was going". She didn't even come to his chin, he guessed her at about five foot four. *Yep, pretty, sassy, and gutsy.* He liked her spunk. Not many women in her position would have popped off like that to a strange man on the side of the road. Especially when that man topped her by a good eight inches.

She hadn't been afraid of him. Her velvety brown eyes had just been reasonably wary. Yep, he liked her spunk. *And her sassy mouth.* Well, those sassy lips anyway.

Megan slid into the booth, taking the seat across from Chad, and a gray-haired waitress appeared with two huge glasses of tea.

"Here ya go, Chadwick," the woman teased.

Her rescuer shot the woman a look and pushed the container of sweeteners in Megan's direction. The waitress walked off chuckling as Megan raised a questioning brow. "Chadwick? Is it a family name or something?"

"Something like that," he muttered.

Megan glanced up at an embarrassed-looking Mrs. Winslow. "Don't look at me," the older woman protested, "I didn't do it, his father did."

A slight flush darkened his tanned cheeks as Chad fidgeted with his glass. "Just drop it, okay."

Nadine sidled up and leaned a hip against the side of the booth by Chad's shoulder. "Family name?" she hooted. "That's not what I heard."

"Nadine . . ."

Ignoring the threat in Chad's voice, the woman ran her hand over the back of his thick black hair in a possessive gesture. "The way I heard it, Buck took one look at his squalling new son, declared the kid bellowed like a bull and promptly named him after his prize Hereford, Chadwick's Lucky Star."

Chad bolted from his seat, his face a deep crimson, and muttering something about needing to make a phone call, made a hasty exit. Nadine's trilling laughter filled the restaurant as she sashayed to the back to pick up her next order.

In the silence that followed, Megan chanced a glance in Mrs. Winslow's direction. Chad's mother shrugged her shoulders helplessly, then suddenly she and Megan both broke into giggles at the same time. Eileen slid into the seat her son had vacated and shook her head. "Poor Chad."

"You mean it's true?" Mrs. Winslow looked startled and Megan quickly added, "About his namesake, I mean."

"I'm afraid so. At the time I didn't see any harm in it, his name is Chad, not Chadwick, but I should have known better. When you live in the same area where you were born and raised, everybody knows your business. There's no keeping any secrets when half the folks are kin to you in one form or another."

"I can imagine. Nadine's related?"

"Nadine's just trouble. Celia's my cousin, though."

"Aha." Megan took a deep drink of her tea.

"Have you booked a place to stay tonight?" Eileen asked.

Meg shook her head. "No, I'd hoped to make it into Houston."

"We probably have a vacancy. Nothing fancy, but it'd be clean and comfortable."

"You have a motel here?"

"This a full-service truck stop, I'll have you know," the older woman announced proudly. "We fill 'em up, wash 'em down, feed the drivers, provide laundry and shower facilities, and have clean comfortable beds."

Two large unkempt men chose that moment to enter the restaurant, laughing loudly. One gave Megan a thorough inspection, then winked at her while the other lightly swatted Nadine in passing. They disappeared into the men's room for a minute then came back out, the winker stopping to activate the jukebox. Nadine hurried to their table with glasses of water and menus and allowed herself to be pulled down onto one man's knee while he gave her his order.

Megan dropped her eyes to the table in front of her and stammered, "Ah, I . . . thanks for the offer, but I think I'd better go on . . ."

"Oh, don't worry about them," Eileen snapped. "That riffraff don't stay here, they're local. Besides, I've got a half dozen rooms away from where the men stay for the women drivers who come through. During the summers some drivers have their families with them too, so I put them in that same section. Those rooms have private baths and you'd be as safe as in your bed at home."

Nadine was back, flirting with the drivers and Eileen shot her a disgusted look. "That is provided you don't go flaunting your assets like some I could name." Her attention returned to Megan and she added, "And I don't believe you're the type to do that."

"No, I don't think so," Megan agreed with a grin.

"Good, it's settled then."

"Thanks." Megan took another sip of her tea and sighed. "Now all I need is a job."

"We have those, too."

Shaking her head, Megan protested, "I wasn't hinting. Just because your son gave me a lift doesn't mean I expect you to adopt me."

Eileen smiled. "I'm looking out for my own interests. We're always in need of willing workers here, but I imagine you're used to doing something more than waiting tables or pumping fuel."

"I've waited a few tables in my time, but my most recent employment was as assistant to the district manager of an electrical parts manufacturer."

"Sounds interesting."

"Not really."

Eileen watched her expectantly, but Megan remained silent and turned her gaze to the window, making it obvious that no more information would be forthcoming.

Eileen cleared her throat. "Well, I don't know what you'll find around here in that line, should be something. But, if you need a job to tide you over . . ."

Megan tilted her head. "Do you really need help or are you just being nice?"

Eileen nodded to a *help wanted* sign posted in the window by the cash register stand. "That's been up for a week now, but I'll tell you true this is no place for tender feelings." She indicated the rough-looking

men in the corner booth. "Most of them aren't like
that, but you'll have to be able to deal with their kind
as well as the ones who're just missing their families
and like to tease a pretty girl."

"Then it isn't a lot different from a large office. Men
are men, whether they need a bath or not, some just
have better manners is all."

Eileen laughed. "I do believe you've got it figgered
out, sugar. You'll do just fine. Celia," she called,
"watch things while I get our newest waitress settled,
will ya?"

*Confound that Nadine! The woman's got no more
sense than a goose in a corn silo. But then what's that
say about you for getting mixed up with her, huh,
Chad old boy?* Slapping his hat against his thigh in
irritation, he went inside the gas station to call a
wrecker for Megan's car, then drove back out to where
they'd left it.

He made a U-turn across the highway and parked
behind the car as before, to await the tow truck. The
abandoned vehicle looked a lot less interesting without
Megan leaning against it.

He pictured her there, her hair flying in the wind of
a passing truck, the sun's golden rays caught in the
honey-toned tendrils that stuck to her face. A few light
freckles sprinkled her nose and more than a little dust
and grit had dusted her cheeks. His smile softened.
Her lips had been all pouted up in disgust at her pre-
dicament, her brows curled over deep brown eyes.

She'd been mussed, flustered, and short tempered. And totally adorable. He sighed and slumped down in the wide bench seat of the old truck.

His mother was right. He hadn't learned his lesson yet, it seemed.

Chapter Two

Megan followed Eileen out of the cafe and into another large building which housed the refueling portion of the operation. It also included a large snack and souvenir shop. Megan discovered Chad had left her luggage behind the counter where a black-haired youth was ringing up a customer's purchase.

Eileen nodded to him then offered the registration book to Megan, choosing a room key while she signed in. "Follow me," she ordered as she picked up the smaller bags and led the way through a back door.

A short corridor ended at a large steel door marked *fire exit only*, and was flanked with three doors on each side. "The men's dorm is on the other side," Eileen said with a jerk of her head toward the steel door. "That can only be opened from this side."

She unlocked the door to a center room and handed Megan the key to a clean but Spartan cubicle. It had a chest with a small television, a double bed, and a nightstand with a lamp and clock radio. A light-blue corded bedspread was turned back to reveal crisp white sheets and the room smelled of fresh linens.

Fat white towels hung in the bathroom, which came equipped with a shower stall instead of a tub, a toilet, and a sink with no vanity. Just the bare necessities, but at the moment, it looked great to Megan.

"Come back over in an hour and we'll get you started," Eileen instructed. "You'll only get minimum wage, but that's more than some of the fancy places pay."

Megan nodded, remembering restaurants could consider tip money as part of a waitress's wages and therefore ignore the minimum wage laws.

She quickly unpacked, then took a long soothing shower. This wasn't quite what she'd planned, but it wasn't so bad either. A roof over her head, a job. When you thought about it, what else did a person really need?

Love? Not hardly!

She pulled on a pair of slim jeans, not nearly so tight as those Nadine wore, and a crisp cotton shirt of pastel plaid. She glanced at her sandals, then dug through another bag to find her sturdy leather athletic shoes. The one thing she remembered vividly about waitressing was the need for good, supportive shoes.

Five minutes ahead of schedule, she presented herself to Eileen. "Ready or not, here I am."

Eileen made a show of looking her over, then
grinned. "You clean up pretty good."

"Gee, thanks."

"Too much camouflage, though, come here."

Eileen grabbed Megan's wrist and pulled her to the
ladies' room. "Tuck in that shirt. I said don't flaunt
your assets, not hide them entirely. You look like a
school teacher."

Megan shook her head in amusement, but followed
orders.

"That's better, now let's roll these sleeves a couple
of turns to show off those pretty arms a little." Eileen
cuffed Megan's short sleeves, then stepped back. She
reached up and flipped the back of Megan's collar up
and unbuttoned the top button. "We're gettin' there,"
she observed. "Got a comb?"

Megan warily produced her comb and Eileen removed the elastic band she'd used to pull her hair
back. She teased Megan's hair, then reached for a
nearby can of spray. She fluffed the hair with her fingers, all the while spraying generously, until Megan
began to cough. When the mist cleared, Megan was
surprised with the results. She'd imagined looking like
the survivor of a tornado, but her hair really looked
quite nice fluffed and full around her face.

Eileen smiled at her in the mirror. "Now all you
need are some really dangly earrings and you'll rake
in the tips."

"Mrs. Winslow—"

"Uh-oh, it's Mrs. Winslow, is it?"

"It's just that I thought this job was waiting tables, I . . ."

Eileen laughed. "Of course that's all it is, but that doesn't mean you have to hide the fact that you're pretty. Believe me, most those ol' boys appreciate a pretty woman who knows how to behave herself a whole lot more than they let on. Reminds them of their wives and sweethearts. Now, just be yourself and don't take no sass."

Chad stepped into the cafe and glanced around, looking for Megan. His mother stood chatting with a couple of drivers as they paid their bill, so he dropped into a booth. In another half hour the place would be busy.

"Good afternoon," greeted a soft voice by his shoulder.

He was assailed by the scent of lilacs as a glass of water and a menu were placed before him. Megan smiled and his gaze fastened on her lips, now glazed with soft rose coloring.

"May I get you something?"

He swallowed and replied, "Uh, not yet thanks. Mom put you to work, huh?"

"It seems she had an opening. Lucky for me."

"Yeah. Is this what you usually do?"

She smiled again. He found he really liked her smile. "Not for awhile, but I haven't had time to check out the need for executive assistants."

"No, I guess not. Oh, your car's fixed."

"You fixed it? Already? That's wonderful, thank you."

The pleasure in her smile and the warmth in her eyes made him wish there were something more he could do for her. Like slay a dragon, or gift-wrap the moon.

"I'll give you what money I have now, and maybe in a couple of days I can repay the rest," she was saying.

He cleared his throat. "Don't worry about it, it came to less than I thought."

Her smile disappeared under a frown. "I can't let you do that."

"Okay," he said evenly, "we'll settle up next week when you get your first paycheck."

Immediately the smile returned. "Great."

Yeah, great, he thought. Here he was doing it again, sticking his neck out. Heck, he wished it was only his neck on the line.

A driver came in and seated himself at one of her tables, so Megan hurried off for water and a menu. He'd laid his cap on the table and was reaching for the wall-mounted telephone beside him when she approached. Chad watched as the man's hand fell still and a wide grin split his weathered face at her greeting. "Afternoon yourself little lady. You're new here ain'tcha?"

"First day," she agreed.

He squinted at her name tag. "Well, Meg, I'll have to be sure I stop by here more often."

"We'll look forward to it," she replied smoothly. "Would you like to order now, or do you need a few minutes to decide?"

"Get me the chicken fried steak with mashed potatoes and plenty of gravy. Keep that rabbit food in the kitchen and give me extra green beans instead."

"You got it. Coffee?"

"Of course!"

"Of course, and how about a thick slice of homemade cherry pie?"

"Sounds good."

"With ice cream melting over it?"

The driver laughed. "You sure know how to make a man's mouth water."

"We aim to please."

Chad was impressed by the smooth way she handled the innocent flirtation as well as the way she'd increased the order. As the evening rush built, he watched her perform with humor and competence, bantering with the customers but always very much the lady. He also noticed that her customers responded to Megan's style of hospitality with generous tips.

"You eating here tonight?"

Chad glanced over at his mother from his perch on a stool behind the register stand. "I might."

"Hmmm."

He started to answer, but his attention swerved to the door. Three ranch hands jostled each other, laughing loudly and cutting up as they ambled in. They took the nearest empty booth, one of Megan's.

"Whoee, lookit here," one of the men crowed as he threw an arm around Megan's waist. "I found me somthin' right tasty for dessert."

"Don't mind him, darlin'," another one drawled, leering at her. "You can have yourself a real man, what time do you get off?" The third just chuckled nastily.

Her face flushed, but Megan remained professional, setting down the water and menus before twisting from the man's hold. "Are you gentlemen ready to order, or would you like a few minutes to study your menus?"

"My, my. A prissy little thing ain't she?"

"It ain't the way she talks that interests me."

"Just a cotton pickin' minute, I saw her first."

She walked off without taking their orders. Chad watched her deliver dinner to two tables before returning and asking pleasantly, "Are you gentlemen ready to order?"

Each told her what he wanted to eat, then one of them managed to swat her when she turned away again. The trio laughed loudly.

A muscle twitched in his jaw, and Chad got slowly to his feet, strolled to the back of the room, and took up a post near the window where the cook set the prepared plates.

* * *

The dinner rush over and the tables wiped down, the day shift waitresses prepared to leave for home, all wishing Megan a good night and giving her good-natured advice and encouragement as they left. All except for Nadine, who hissed, "Don't expect to be getting special treatment all the time. Chad don't work here, you know."

Megan had no idea what that meant, but was too tired to worry about it. She'd been up since six this morning, and just wanted to crawl into bed. She slumped into a booth and started to help Eileen roll change. Along one side of the room, the teen-aged boy she'd seen earlier in the mini-market piled chairs on tables so he could mop the floor.

Eileen glanced up from counting the coins. "You okay?"

"Um-hmm, just tired. It's been a long day and I'm not used to such a workout anymore."

"Well, you did fine. I'm pleased to have you on the crew."

"Thanks. I picked it up again quicker than I thought I would."

Eileen grinned. "Like riding a bicycle?"

"I suppose." Megan chuckled then sobered. "Oh, someone delivered orders to one of my tables though and I don't know who. I wanted to thank her."

Eileen returned her attention to the coins. "Oh?"

"Yes. There were three wise guys together and I was dreading it."

"Those boys hail from the Bar K Ranch. Chad took them their supper."

"What?"

Eileen looked up, her expression thoughtful. "Chad took them their supper," she repeated.

"Why?"

"I'm not real sure."

Megan groaned in appreciation as relaxing water sluiced over her tired shoulders and down her back. There might not be a tub to soak in, but hot water was in abundant supply. The thick towels were another unexpected luxury. She dried off and took two aspirin before digging out her hair dryer. Finally sliding between the sweet-smelling sheets, she sighed contentedly and closed her eyes, immediately on the edge of sleep. A sharp rap at the door startled her.

To her relief she found the door outfitted with a peep hole. Chad stood on the other side. She pulled the door open. "Yes?"

He took note of her knee-length sleep shirt printed with negative comments about men, and grinned. "Nice outfit."

"If I'd known the fashion police would be making house calls I'd have worn my silk peignoir," she retorted.

His expression took on a definitely interested look and he offered, "Okay, I'll wait."

She laughed. "In your dreams, cowboy. Now why did you wake me?"

"I forgot to return your car keys." He tossed the keys in the air, caught them, then handed them over. "Thought you might need them in the morning."

"Thanks, but I plan to sleep until ten-thirty. My shift begins at eleven and I'm not getting up one minute before I have to."

"I hear that. Well, sorry I woke you."

"That's all right. Good night."

His gaze fixed on her mouth and he stood motionless for several seconds before the tip of his tongue darted out to moisten his own lips. His body swayed an imperceptible quarter inch towards her and she saw him swallow thickly before he murmured, "Good night, Megan," and turned on his heel.

She stared after him, stunned, her mouth tingling as though she'd been thoroughly kissed when he hadn't even touched her. Not physically anyway.

Closing the door, she staggered back a couple of steps and dropped to a corner of the bed, the keys fisted tightly in her hand. Oh, she'd been touched alright, and she knew it. "Please, Lord," she moaned, "I don't need this, not again."

The keys cut into her hand and when she glanced down at them, the biggest quotation on her night shirt caught her eye. *How do you know when a man is lying? His lips are moving.* "Ain't it the truth," she whispered, and climbed back into bed, seeking refuge under the light covers.

But was that Chad? Would he be like Harry? He seems so decent, so unselfish. Unbidden, his image filled her mind's eye. Dark, dark hair ruffled by the wind danced on his forehead. One tan, muscular arm propped on the truck's window sill, the opposite wrist draped over the top of the big steering wheel in that relaxed, masculine way. Humor sparkled in the depths of his indigo eyes. The shoulder that had occupied the space several inches from her own, strained against the seams of his soft cotton tee shirt. A shirt which followed the tapering lines of his torso into the waist-band of slim denims. No beer gut on that cowboy, no sir.

She permitted herself a gusty sigh. A girl could easily get used to having someone like Chad around.

Chapter Three

A gray-haired trucker in crisp jeans and neat western shirt doffed his hat and held the restaurant door open for Megan. Eileen looked up and smiled. "Mornin'. Wondered if you'd get here in time to grab a bite before clocking in."

"I hadn't meant to, but I suppose I should eat something."

"You'd better, otherwise you won't get the chance for nearly three hours. Can't have my waitresses passing out from hunger."

Megan laughed and went to the back to ask the cook to scramble her up some eggs. She paused at the coffee urn to fill a cup.

"Well la-te-da," a female voice drawled.

"Hello, Nadine." The younger woman stood with a

hand on a cocked hip, insolently looking Megan up and down. "Is there a problem?"

"Not from where I stand," Nadine jeered, then walked off.

Megan carried her coffee to the front where Eileen sat in a booth. "What's with her?"

"Don't bother about Nadine."

"Isn't this suitable for work?" she asked, indicating her outfit.

"Well of course it is. Too good actually. It'd be a shame to stain those nice slacks."

Megan shrugged. "They're just wash and wear."

She ate a hasty breakfast, then set to work giving all her tables a quick wipedown, making certain each held an ashtray and salt and pepper shakers.

Chad entered and glanced around, quickly spotting Megan polishing a table. Her hair was fluffed into a golden cloud and she bit one corner of her full lower lip in concentration. Near his shoulder an amused voice greeted, "Good morning, son."

He started guiltily and turned. "Hi, Mom."

Eileen shook her head slowly. "Chad, Chad, Chad."

He gritted his teeth and waited for a lecture, but his mother only patted his cheek and walked off.

"Hi."

He turned back to Megan. "Hi yourself. Did you get your sleep?"

"Yes I did. I think I can join the land of the living today."

"Well, you certainly look ready to take on the world," he teased.

She wrinkled her nose at him and laughed. "May I get you some coffee?"

"Thanks, but I wait on myself around here."

"I don't mind, really."

"Okay, tell Sam I'd like a plate of eggs with hash browns too, if you would."

"Boy, give 'em an inch and they take a mile," Megan grouched good-naturedly.

The tables were starting to fill with the lunch crowd when Chad called out to her, "See you later."

She gave him a distracted wave and continued taking a customer's order. For the next two and a half hours business kept her much too busy to think of anything else.

The women sat at two tables, taking a well-deserved break. Nadine slouched alone in a booth, her cigarette dangling from beringed fingers, pointedly ignoring Megan. An elderly woman, no more than five feet tall and about seventy pounds of sharp bones and weathered skin, shuffled over and sat down across from Megan. Her wrinkled face drew up in a gap-toothed grin and she greeted, "Howdy, I'm Alma. Welcome to The Depot."

Megan smiled at the tiny white-haired woman. "I know who you are, your reputation precedes you."

"What?" Alma squawked. "Lies, all lies! I ain't seduced a man in more years than I can remember."

Megan looked startled and Eileen started laughing. "Alma, behave yourself," she scolded fondly, "the girl don't know how to take you yet. She's talking about your baking and you know it."

"Oh that," Alma replied smugly.

"Yes that," Megan chuckled, warming to the old woman at once. "I'm Meg, Megan Stallings."

Alma cackled and threw a sly look towards Nadine. "Yeah, I know. You're Chad's new girl."

Nadine snarled a cutting name under her breath and viciously crushed out her cigarette.

Alma cackled gleefully at the girl's departing back while Megan recovered enough to protest, "I'm no such thing, I just met the man. He only gave me a ride . . ." but no one seemed to pay her disclaimers any attention.

It didn't help the situation when Chad chose that moment to come in and offer, "If you can spare Megan for a little while I'll show her around the place."

Alma's renewed cackle overrode the other women's snickers and Megan wished for a hole in which to hide. Eileen smiled and answered, "Sure, give her the grand tour."

He stood looking down at Megan, hands on his hips. "Well, are you up to it?"

While the others struggled to suppress their mirth, Alma had no such qualms. The old woman's bony frame shook as Megan slid from the booth, a surge of heat climbing her face. "That'd be great, let's go," she gritted. Anything to get out of here!

"What was that all about?" he asked as soon as they were outside.

"Nothing."

"That bad, huh? Well don't let 'em get to you. When Aunt Alma starts in teasing, you know you've won her approval. It makes you one of the 'in crowd', a member of the family."

Megan couldn't help laughing, then shook her head ruefully. "Gee thanks, I think."

Chad grinned. "Anytime." He slipped his hand under her hair and cupped the back of her neck, steering her towards the fuel pumps with a gentle pressure. It was an intimate, possessive gesture, but she didn't protest, instead finding the warm contact reassuring.

With a flourish of his free hand, he presented the islands of gasoline and diesel pumps. "Here we have the heart of a truck stop operation, the fuel pumps. There are some, however, like Mom, who insist the coffee urn is the first priority and diesel second."

A large moving van pulled in just then and an attractive girl came bustling out of the mini-mart building to fuel it. Insulated coffee bottle in hand, the driver swung down from his cab and headed for the cafe.

"Looks like a toss-up to me," Megan observed.

"Yeah, I guess it is at that." Chad grinned, then turned her in the direction the pump girl had come from.

Behind the counter, a tall man talked on the phone, ordering supplies. He looked up when they entered and smiled, and Megan realized this must be Chad's

father. Looking at the older man, she knew she was
seeing Chad in about twenty-five years. A light sprin-
kling of silver threaded the older man's hair at the
temples, glistening against the ebony strands. His face
had a few more character lines and his body was
thicker, but the warmth of his smile and the sparkle in
his eyes mirrored his son's exactly.

"Well, well," he greeted as he hung up the phone,
his voice jovial and warm, "it's about time you
brought her in." He held out a large hand to Megan.
"I'm Buck Winslow, Chad's old man."

"Are you?" Megan teased. "I'd have guessed you
were his brother."

"Younger or older?" he fired back.

"Younger, of course."

Buck threw back his head and roared in appreciative
laughter, then swore, "You've hit the jackpot this time
boy, you surely have." He grinned at Megan. "It's a
pure pleasure to meet you, gal."

She realized Chad was beaming down on her
proudly when she felt his hand squeeze her waist. "I'd
have brought her over sooner," he told his father, "but
Mom put her to work right away."

"That so?"

"Yeah, she worked the dinner shift last night and
lunch today. I had to kidnap her just now to get her
away from that flock of hens over there."

Buck chuckled and shook his head. "Watch how
you talk, son, you don't want to rile them gals, or we
won't be able to get a decent meal for a week."

Chad gave Megan a mock look of concern. "You won't squeal on us, will you?"

She just shook her head, aware of the warm intimacy of the hand that continued to grip her waist.

"Too bad Eileen got to you first," Buck told her. "I could have used you on the pump islands. Of course with tips, you get paid better over there."

"And it's air conditioned," Megan pointed out.

"Not from around here, are you?" Buck teased.

"She's from Kansas," Chad supplied. "Blew in on a tornado."

Megan jabbed an elbow into his ribs. "Ow."

"Well, if she's headed for Oz look out," Buck muttered, "here comes the wicked witch."

Nadine jerked open the heavy glass door and slapped money down on the counter. Without a word between them, Buck flipped her a pack of cigarettes and she stalked out again, but not before giving Megan a malevolent glare.

"Whew," Buck whistled, "I do believe the battle lines are drawn."

"I don't know why she hates me," Megan mused, "but she does."

Buck's startled gaze flew from his son to Megan and back, but at a frown from Chad, the older man held his peace.

"To get back to your tour," Chad said, "as I told you outside, this is the hub of the operation. Dad oversees the servicing of the trucks, the washing booths, and the mini-market here."

"And most times, the renting of beds," Buck added.

Chad looked at Megan. "Which reminds me, is your room okay?"

"It's fine, why?"

"I noticed Mom put you in the middle where you'd have more quiet, but do you have everything you need?"

She couldn't help it, her heart skipped a beat at that question, voiced softly with an expression of true concern. *Almost everything*, she thought, *almost*. "Yes, of course." Then she gave a nervous little laugh. "I mean, I have my health, a roof over my head, a job, plenty to eat, and my car is running—I still owe you for that, by the way—most of which I didn't have at this time yesterday. What more could a person ask?"

Chad's gaze drifted to her lips and she again had the uncanny feeling of having been kissed without being touched. Her face heated and she wanted to look away, but Chad's gaze came back up to hold hers, and it occurred to her that she'd never seen blue eyes look so heated. Like ink about to boil. She caught her breath in a quiet little gasp.

The van driver came in to pay his bill, breaking the spell, and she moved quickly from the counter. Turning her back on Chad, she struggled to regain her composure. She didn't need this, she just didn't need this! *Please*, she begged her ricocheting heart, *don't do this to me, not again!*

She jumped when Chad took her elbow. "Come on, I'll show you the rest of the place."

Outside, Chad gestured to a tall open-ended structure. "Back here is the wash area, and that's Jamie."

The youth Megan had seen mopping the cafe last night was busy sweeping mud and debris from the concrete floor of a washing stall. A small boy stood to one side, watching him. Jamie waved and the child turned and saw them.

"Mr. Chad, see my new horse," the boy called as he launched himself into a run. Short legs churning, toy held aloft, he barreled in their direction.

"Carlos!" Chad and Jamie both yelled at the same time.

The boy skidded to a halt and froze in place. Eyes wide and startled, he looked around him, then his shoulders slumped. Chad reached the small figure in only a few long strides and hunkered down on his heels, one large hand on the child's shoulder.

"I forgot," Megan heard the little boy mutter.

"Yes, you did," Chad answered sternly. "You can't forget, Carlos, you know that."

"I know."

"What happens if you forget?" Chad prompted.

"I can't come here no more."

"That's right, and we don't want that, do we?"

"No." Carlos scuffed at the asphalt with the toe of his sneaker.

Chad straightened and held out a hand which the child readily took. "Come over here, there's someone I'd like you to meet."

The boy looked both ways, leaning around Chad's

frame to do so, and Megan realized he'd just been chastised for running headlong across an area frequented by the huge tractor-trailer rigs which were the truck stop's main business. Vehicles whose drivers might not see a small child dart among the massive frames.

The large plastic horse clutched securely to his chest, the boy took exaggerated strides, trying his best to match Chad's shortened steps. They stopped before her and Chad dropped the small hand. "Megan, I'd like you to meet Carlos Mendeola. Carlos, this is Miss Megan Stallings."

She took the extended hand and shook it. "I'm pleased to meet you, Carlos."

"Me too," he answered gravely, then immediately offered up the horse for her inspection. "See my new horse? Jamie got it for me, it's a Paint."

She took the brown and white replica and studied it carefully. "So it is, and a beautifully marked one at that."

"Yeah," he agreed with a vigorous shake of his head.

"Carlos collects horses," Chad explained. "He plans on raising them when he finishes school."

He again dropped to his haunches in front of the child. "Speaking of which, how is life in the second grade?"

"Okay," the boy said with a shrug, "but we're doing the same things we did *last* year. Letters and numbers, letters and numbers."

Chad laughed. "Well it's important to get those things down, you know. You've learned to read new words, haven't you?"

"I guess," Carlos admitted with a sigh.

"See? It's not quite the same after all."

Carlos just wrinkled his nose in answer. Megan handed him back the horse.

"How many is that now?" Chad asked.

The small black eyebrows drew together in concentration. "Three I think. No, four. I have a Palomino, a Quarter Horse, a App'loosa, and now a Paint."

Chad emitted a low whistle. "You're getting quite a herd there, partner."

"Not a *real* one."

"I know." Chad patted the dark head. "That will come in time though. I spotted a nice Arabian the other day. Study hard and when you get your first report card we'll see about adding him to your stable."

Eyes alight with pleasure, Carlos answered, "All right!" Then the slender shoulders slumped again. "But that's a long time away," he protested.

Chad laughed. "No it isn't, just three or four weeks. That's barely enough time for you to make sure you've got those letters and numbers down pat."

"Carlos," Jamie called from across the lot, "time to go."

"See you," the child wheeled away, then caught himself and paused to check for traffic before running to his brother's side.

As Megan watched him go, Chad straightened to

his feet beside her. Mere inches separated them. She caught his special scent, spice and sun-warmed cotton, and an awkward silence settled in the space vacated by the little boy's animated chatter.

Megan cleared her throat. "Your mother wasn't kidding when she said this is a full-service facility," she said, searching for something to break the escalating tension.

Chad's glance flicked over her face. A slight lifting of his lips told her he wasn't fooled by her tactic. "I guess I'd better get you back," he said quietly.

They walked behind the buildings, not touching, their steps slow. Only a fool or inexperienced girl wouldn't recognize the signs of a man's interest, and Megan was neither. Well, not inexperienced, anyway. She paused as they reached the corner of the building and laid a hand on Chad's arm. How did one put a stop to something that hadn't really started?

"Chad?"

His gaze met hers in a look more heated than before. As she watched, a pained expression crossed his face. "Megan," he whispered, and the next thing she knew, he'd drawn her into his arms. His mouth covered any protest.

She'd barely recovered from her surprise when he stepped back, releasing her for only a moment, his large hands bracketing her face. He studied her eyes for a heartbeat, while she struggled for something to say, but before the words of denial could form, he pulled her to him again.

When Chad ended the kiss, he continued to hold her close. Pressed that tightly to his chest, Megan felt the hammer-blows of his heart, while her own raced so wildly it made her light-headed. Though fierce, his embrace wasn't uncomfortable, but reassuring and she had a distinct impression of . . . rightness? Completeness? Of coming home.

He eased his hold and gently set her from him. "Sorry," he whispered hoarsely, "guess I got a little carried away."

She nodded her bent head once and heard him sigh before he took her lightly by the shoulders and kissed her hair. "You'd better go in," he murmured, then turned abruptly and strode off in the direction from which they'd come.

Drawing a long shaky breath, she watched him go. *Just like that? She was supposed to go back in there and resume her work just like that? The man had to be crazy!*

Unconsciously covering her lips with trembling fingers, she tried for a steadying breath. With his long strides, he was almost to the end of the building and she knew without a doubt he'd turn to look at her when he reached it.

She couldn't be staring after him when he did, she just couldn't. Spinning quickly on her heel, she rounded the corner.

She slipped in through the kitchen door and managed to avoid everyone on her way to the ladies' room. There, she splashed her face with cold water several times before patting it dry. She pulled a lipstick from her pocket and dashed it across her trembling mouth. After fluffing her hair with her fingertips she sprayed it again, then carefully judged her reflection.

Her world had just been violently shaken and spilled out at her feet. Did it show? Would anyone be able to tell what she'd been doing? Surely her lips were burned with the imprint of his kisses? Megan studied the startled woman in the mirror. The reflection stared back silently; the wide eyes and quivering mouth dismally unreassuring.

Chad's long strides carried him quickly to the far end of the long building. He slowed as he reached the corner and glanced over his shoulder at the way he'd come, but Megan was gone. He rounded the corner and stopped abruptly. One hand reached out to the cinder block wall for support. He dropped his head and concentrated on drawing slow even breaths in an attempt to calm his racing heart.

For Pete's sake, how did that happen? You just met the woman, you don't know a thing about her. Except that she's running from something. A woman like that doesn't drive all the way from Kansas in a rickety little car with just a couple of boxes and her suitcases unless she's running away. She's a lady with a problem and you can't save the world. Haven't you learned your lesson? Chad shook his head in disgust, lifted his hat and ran shaky fingers through his hair. He needed to think.

More slowly, he continued up the side of the building to where he'd parked his truck. Climbing in, he ignored his father's beckoning gesture from the other side of the plate glass, and started the engine. With deliberate care, he backed the old pickup out and turned it toward the ranch. He wouldn't think of Megan anymore until he got there—he didn't need to find himself in a ditch or against a tree.

South of town he left the highway, for once oblivious to the beauty of the gently rolling terrain, the sturdy oak trees that provided umbrellas of shade to lush pastures, the fat cattle dozing in the afternoon heat. Attention fixed firmly on the road ahead, he sat upright in his seat, both hands clutching the wheel with the determination of a beginning driver.

Car on the right waiting to enter the roadway. Oncoming truck, watch for cars trying to pass.

By focusing on his driving with single-minded purpose he managed to keep thoughts of Megan at bay until he drove through the gates of the Rocking W Ranch.

He pulled to a stop in front of the white clapboard house. Puffs of dust rose from the dirt and gravel drive to cloud around the tires. He shut off the engine, removed his hat and slumped down in the seat. Lordy, lordy, what had he done?

You've fallen in love, you idiot, practically at first sight. Just like your father and his father before him. "That's what I was afraid of," he confirmed aloud to himself. "And I'm not even free to do anything about it."

Chapter Four

Megan emerged from the washroom prepared to give the best performance of her life, but Eileen took one look at her and hurried over. "The girls have the restaurant under control, come give me a hand making up the rooms, would you?"

Megan followed her out, but stopped Eileen just outside the mini-market door. "I've just seen the rooms, they're all made up, Eileen."

"I know, I just thought you might need a little more time to collect yourself."

Megan blushed but remained silent.

"Those ladies could tree a bobcat with their teasing once they get their teeth into something," Eileen clarified, but Megan detected anxiety under the forced heartiness.

"Thank you."

"You're welcome. Now let's go back here and pretend we're making beds for a few minutes."

Unlocking a room next to Megan's, Eileen sat on the edge of a bunk bed, motioning her to sit on the double bed. Obviously, this was one of the family rooms. "So, how are you liking it here so far?" Eileen asked a little too brightly.

Megan smiled at the older woman's attempt to put her at ease. "I like it fine, thank you. I can't begin to repay you for your kindness, taking me in like you did."

"Oh, pooh! You're a hard worker, I'm grateful to have you."

Megan smiled her thanks for the compliment, then fixed her employer with a steady gaze. "What is it you really want to say, Eileen?"

The blue eyes looked startled for a moment, then crinkled as Eileen chuckled. "I guess I'm about as transparent as you are." She took a deep breath and blurted out, "What do you think of my son?"

It was Megan's turn to look startled and a humiliated flush began to climb her neck. What must this woman think of her? She'd arrived barely twenty-four hours ago and already seemed on the verge of some kind of relationship with the woman's son! But a glance at Eileen's expression told Megan she really wanted an answer, so she dropped her gaze and murmured, "I think Chad is the most considerate man I've ever met."

Eileen waited, obviously not satisfied with a partial answer.

"I like him. A lot."

"Good." Eileen exhaled as though she'd been holding her breath. "I'm glad to hear it. Just try not to let it show too much around the cafe."

Megan nodded in agreement, leaving unvoiced all the questions which Eileen's request posed.

When they returned to the restaurant, Nadine shot her a suspicious look, but Megan pretended not to notice. Before leaving for the evening though, that woman passed close to her and warned through gritted teeth, "Stay away from Chad."

Obviously, Nadine had her eye on Chad, but surely she didn't hope to win him simply by scaring off the competition? More puzzling was Chad's absence. When he didn't appear for supper, Megan thought he'd probably stop by at the end of her shift, but he failed to materialize then, too.

"What did you expect?" she muttered to herself as she unlocked the door to her room. "You practically crawl into his pocket within a day of meeting a man, and he's not going to think too highly of you." Not that she wanted him to, she told herself. She wasn't interested in that kind of complication.

She dropped to the edge of the bed and unlaced her shoes. Prying them off with her toes, she flopped back on the mattress with a groan. A long soak in a hot tub would sure feel good to her aching muscles, but she'd have to make do with the shower. Not that she was complaining. She appreciated her cramped accommodations more than the Winslows could ever imagine.

If she chose, she could hole up in Huntsville, Texas, for the rest of her life. No one would ever find her here. Not Harry, not his wife, not even that blood-thirsty school of reporters. Which reminded her, she needed to call her parents. They'd be worried that she hadn't checked in with them in a couple of days.

A steamy shower loosened her tired body, and with a grateful sigh she slipped between crisp sheets, propped herself on the pillows, and reached for the book she'd bought from Buck after work. The mini-market didn't have a wide selection, but she'd found one by her favorite romance author, though now she doubted the wisdom of her choice. The very last thing she needed was to entertain thoughts of a romantic nature! She sighed again and opened the book, quickly reading the first page, then the second.

"Oh great," she grumbled as she read the passage in which the heroine met her protagonist. "The hero looks like Chad."

The description listed "hair the color of a raven's wing, eyes of darkest indigo, shoulders the breadth of an axe handle and a half." She added silently to herself, "and kisses that could woo the angels from the sky. Darn."

The book dropped to her lap and she gave herself up to the activity she'd tried to avoid all afternoon; thinking of Chad Winslow. The way he smiled, the way she felt whenever he was near . . . the way he'd kissed her. Ah, yes, the way he'd kissed her. Unconsciously, her fingertips drifted to her lips as though to feel that kiss again.

Headlights bounced lightly up the road, sweeping the front porch as the late model Suburban curved into the driveway. Chad sat motionless in a corner of the darkened porch as his parents mounted the steps of the family home. His mother paused at the top. "You didn't come in to dinner."

"No ma'am," he answered quietly.

"Do you mind if I ask why?"

"I don't always take my meals there, do I?" he evaded.

"No," his mother agreed, "but somehow I expected you."

Buck kissed Eileen's cheek and crossed to the door, his boot heels echoing on the wood planks. "G'night, son."

" 'Night."

The spring on the screen squealed, then snapped the door shut in the big man's wake. Eileen remained poised at the edge of the porch. "Do you want to talk?"

"About what?"

"About whatever's bothering you."

How did she know these things, he wondered. "Not yet, Mom, okay?"

Eileen walked to the corner where he sat in an old painted rocking chair and touched his hair. "Okay, honey. But you know I'm always ready to listen. Same for your daddy. We'll do whatever we can to help, you know that."

"I know, Mom. Thanks."

Through the screen door Chad could hear his parents' muted voices as they climbed the stairs together. A moment later a soft rectangle of light fell from their bedroom window onto the yard below, then all went dark again as someone pulled the shade.

Tomorrow, Chad thought, *I'll call my lawyer again first thing tomorrow.*

Megan sat bolt upright and stared hard at the shadowed walls, momentarily disoriented. Her heart raced, struggling in her chest like a panicked bird, and her lungs labored to draw oxygen from quick shallow breaths.

Awakened by the realism of her nightmare, events of the past several days swirled through her sleep-fogged mind, then slowly coalesced. With a groan, she eased herself back down onto her pillow and focused her attention on breathing deeply, slowly, in an effort to relax her trembling body.

The dream had begun disturbingly enough with her warmly ensconced in Chad's arms, his lips lowering gently to hers. Suddenly Harry's face, not Chad's loomed above her and in the background his wife screeched, "You'll pay for this, Harry, this time you'll pay!"

Warm tears slid down Megan's cheeks as a humiliated flush climbed her body in the darkened room.

There was no one here who witnessed her disgrace, but she felt it just the same. She'd been infatuated with a first-class heel.

Her charming, attentive boss had been her first serious crush. She'd been wooed by the flattery of the handsome, older man and easy prey to his manipulation.

She dropped a forearm over her eyes. How could she have been so stupid? Though she'd resisted going out with him while he was still married, she'd believed every age-old cliche he'd trotted out. *"My marriage is over, we're only housemates now." "You must know you're very special to me."*

This went on for nearly a year before Megan had bumped into a smiling Mrs. Thomas coming out of Harry's office. Megan had been further shocked to note that the woman appeared to be around five months pregnant. Housemates, indeed!

She could almost forgive herself her gullibility if Harry hadn't gone one better. Not only had he deceived Megan about his wife, he'd cheated on the company. His father-in-law's company. Harry had embezzled several thousands of dollars, and it was about to be discovered. He came to Megan in desperation.

"You have to help me out," he'd argued. "After all, it's partially your fault. If I hadn't become interested in you," he'd continued huskily, "I'd still be with my wife."

Megan didn't bother pointing out that he obviously was still very much "with" the clueless Mrs. Thomas but asked instead, "What has any of that to do with the fact you stole from the company?"

"It wasn't really stealing," he'd replied smoothly. "Don't you see? My wife is an only child, it will all be hers someday. I only used some of her money to give her the things she wanted. The house, the car, the trips."

Megan doubted that Mrs. Thomas really wanted the frequent trips to Las Vegas where rumor had it Harry dropped large amounts of cash, or the impossibly priced sports car he drove with the reckless disregard of an eighteen-year-old, but held her peace. "What do you expect me to do, Harry?"

"If you really care about me, I expect you to help me out. Loan me what you can, I'll pay it back, you know I will."

Megan punched her pillow and groaned aloud. Stupid! How could any one woman be so incredibly stupid? But she knew exactly how. She'd wanted to believe, so she'd fallen for one more line.

He'd softened his approach and pulled her into his arms, whispering, "I can't bear the thought of being without you, Megan. You know how much I need you." She'd pushed free of his embrace, maintaining her stand against involvement with a married man. No matter what he promised, he was still married and she'd refused to date him or to permit even the most chaste of intimacies as long as that were true. But that didn't mean she was immune to his entreaties.

Her hands came up to cover her face in an effort to

hide from herself in the darkened room. "Idiot," she muttered. She couldn't bear the thought of him locked up in jail. She'd given Harry all her ready cash that day; her savings, the balance in her checking account, even the coins from the jar in the kitchen.

It wouldn't be nearly enough. He'd sell his car, he said, could she raise any more somehow? In the ensuing weeks she'd sold off most of her furnishings and the small patio home she'd acquired only six months before. She could move back with her parents for a little while.

She handed the proceeds over to Harry, believing he'd use the money to pay on his debt. And of course, she cancelled plans to replace her old car. She didn't have the down payment for a new one now anyway. But at least they could work on straightening out this mess. Or so she'd thought. *Dumb, dumb, dumb!*

Three days after she'd given him the last of the cash, Harry skipped town with his father-in-law's secretary.

Rolling over, she snuggled deeper into the bed like a child hiding from things that go bump in the night, and thought Harry Thomas outranked the bogey man any day.

But Chad, a little voice whispered, now *there* was a man to warm a lady's heart. A true knight of old, clad in denim and a Stetson hat instead of armor, and mounted on an old pickup truck, he rode to the rescue with just the right amount of masculine strength and a whole load of charm.

Megan frowned in the darkness. *Oh, for Pete's sake! That's just what you need, to lose your head again over someone you hardly know.*

The little voice fell silent.

Bright sunlight glowed around the edges of the blinds. Megan yawned and stretched. A glance at the bedside clock told her it was nearly noon. She snuggled deeper into her bed.

Eileen had given her today off, saying Mondays could be her set day off and that her other day would be a rotating one. This week it would be Wednesday. She'd lay here just a little longer, she told herself. At two o'clock she woke again. Three-quarters of an hour later, she walked into the cafe.

"Hello, there," Eileen greeted. "Been busy finding your way around town?"

Megan shook her head. "Actually, I just got up," she admitted.

"That's a relief, I thought you'd taken your meals with some of my competition."

"No way, and I'm starving."

"Well, now that you're rested up, go get some nourishment. Sam has a crock of chicken salad back there that's just plain mouth-watering."

"Sounds good. When I've eaten though, I need to do a little shopping."

"Be glad to show you around if you want the company," Eileen offered.

"Thanks, I'd appreciate it."

* * *

The dinner rush was in full swing by the time they got back and Eileen hurried in to take over the cashiering chores from Celia. Megan carried her purchases— two pair of jeans, four blouses, and some toiletries— to her room, waving to Buck as she passed through the mini-mart. She didn't emerge again until nearly seven-thirty.

"Well, did you girls buy out the stores this afternoon?" Buck teased.

"Hardly, I just needed a couple of things to wear for work, and Eileen went along as guide."

"That's good. If you haven't eaten, how about keeping me company for supper?"

"I'm headed that way now." Megan flashed the older man a smile. "Your wife isn't the jealous type is she?"

"Afraid not." Buck shook his head, his expression woeful. "She's got me hog-tied and she knows it."

"That's the way it should be," Megan replied quietly. "If you love someone, you should be honest and up-front about it. You shouldn't play games."

Buck glanced her way. "Right you are." Then he called out to Jamie, who was stocking the shelves with more potato chips, "Jamie, take over here, while I escort this pretty lady to dinner."

Eileen joined them, and for the first time in ages, Megan felt part of a family. As they ate, the Winslows talked about the town, their business concerns, family and friends. Megan should have seen it coming, but was so relaxed she'd let down her guard.

"So what brought you to Texas?" Buck asked.

She sat in stunned silence, trying frantically to formulate an answer that wouldn't be a lie, but wouldn't diminish her in these people's regard. "I, ah, wanted a change of scenery." *Fantastic, Meg, that has to be the greatest answer in the world!*

Out of the corner of her eye, she caught the movement as Eileen jabbed an elbow into her husband. Buck didn't flinch, just nodded and said, "Well, you picked a good place. Hope you like it enough to stick around awhile."

Megan let out the breath she'd been holding. "Thank you."

"Got room for one more?" Megan jumped at the deep voice, unexpected and so close to her shoulder.

"Always," Buck replied, grinning at his son. "Scoot over, Meg, so we men don't have to talk crossways over you women."

Megan felt herself flushing, but slid over in the booth to give Chad a seat beside her. This was the first she'd seen of him since that shattering kiss, and her heart was bouncing off her ribs.

"Looks like you got here a little late, Chad, what can I get you?" Celia asked as she cleared away the empty plates.

"Nothing, thanks, I grabbed a bite at home."

"Then how about some coffee and dessert?" Eileen offered.

"I wanted to take Megan for a ride, show her around a little. I thought we could stop for an ice cream or something later."

"Show her around?" Buck interjected. "It's getting dark out there." This time he grunted when his wife's elbow made contact.

Megan could feel Chad's gaze on her, but continued to toy with her water glass.

"What do you say, want to see the night lights of Huntsville?"

She tried to match his light tone. "You mean besides the ones across the highway?"

He grinned at her reference to the brightly lit state prison complex nearby. "Yeah, besides them."

She couldn't think of a graceful refusal. "Why not." Why not, indeed! She really hadn't wanted to refuse.

Chad held the door for her when they left the cafe, then slid his hand into hers as they walked to the truck. His palm was hard and warm, calloused from his daily toil. She glanced at their joined hands, hers swallowed in the grip of his much larger one, and wondered at the rightness of it.

"You really don't need to do this, your mother took me around this afternoon. We went shopping."

He leaned on the truck door he'd opened for her. "Oh? Well maybe we'll skip town then and see some of the countryside."

Megan swallowed. "Ah, no, that's okay. If you want to drive through town that's fine. I still don't know my way around."

He swung the old vehicle onto the highway, handling the oversized steering wheel with easy familiarity. The warm evening air poured through their open windows, stirring the scent of warm skin and spicy aftershave around in the cab.

Chad reached across the seat for her hand and tugged. "Don't lean on that door, the latch isn't too reliable."

She scooted a couple of inches from the door. He tugged on her hand again, but she stayed put.

He glanced her way. "What's the matter?"

"Nothing, why?"

"Then what are you doing way over there?"

"Chad . . ."

"You're not afraid of me, are you?"

"Of course not."

"Then what?"

"You move a little fast. After all, we've just met."

His thumb toyed with hers for a moment and a puzzled frown curled his brows. "Yeah, I guess we have at that. But for me, it's like I've known you all my life."

She looked up sharply. Not that she didn't understand what he meant. She'd never felt such an instant rapport with anyone before, either. If it weren't for needing to fight this overwhelming attraction, she'd be completely at ease with him.

"Do you really want to drive around town?" he asked.

"No, I should be turning in soon. I have the early shift tomorrow."

"Let me show you the ranch first," he suggested.

"I don't think that's a good idea."

"Sure it is, besides, Mom and Dad will be there soon, we'll be chaperoned," he teased.

Megan sighed in defeat. "Oh, all right, if it's not too far."

She was instantly sorry she'd yielded as Chad leaned sideways, locked a strong arm around her and scooped her across the seat. Settling her against his hip, he flashed her a charming grin. "Nope, not far at all, about a twenty-minute drive." Then he smiled like a man contented with the world.

They rode in silence for several minutes as Megan attempted to combat the effects of his proximity. She held her body stiff, refusing to relax under the curve of his arm.

He laid his cheek against her hair and moved it in a gentle caress. She closed her eyes. He kissed her forehead, and she melted against him. He squeezed her shoulder, then slid his arm down to catch her waist, holding her snugly to his side.

"Chad?"

"Humm?"

"I think you'd better take me back."

"I will."

"Now."

"I'd really like for you to see the home place."

"But it's dark out."

"There's a moon, see?"

As if on cue, the pristine disc slid from behind a high cloud. *Oh great, just what you need, moonlight and a delicious man. If that doesn't spell trouble I don't know what does.*

She sighed in defeat and Chad whispered, "That's my girl," before kissing her temple.

Chapter Five

They pulled off the highway and crossed a cattle guard flanked by iron posts. The gateway was topped with an arch in which a large W, underscored by a curved bar, was mounted. Metal silhouettes flanked the ranch brand, a cowboy on horseback on one side and a steer heading away on the other.

Half a mile ahead, Megan could see a cluster of buildings illuminated by a rural yard light. Slightly apart, just outside the circle of light, a white frame house peeked from between its sentinel oaks, the painted surface glowing softly under the moon.

The graveled road climbed towards the house, but Chad took a dirt cut-off around the base of the rise.

"Where are we going?"

"I want to show you my favorite spot, over by the big tank."

"Tank?"

He grinned down at her. "Watering hole, cow pond, whatever you call them in Kansas."

The truck bounced along over the rough track, ascending another of the small rolling hills that undulated across this part of the country. When they reached the top, Chad pulled up by a large willow tree and shut off the engine.

"What do you think?" he asked. Stretched before them was a large pond carved into the side of the knoll. Beyond it, hills of descending size rolled away to a meadow. The brilliant moon cut a silver swath across the water and painted the scene below with fragile light. Hereford cattle dotted the pastures, their white faces luminescent in the wash of moonlight. Wide spreading oak trees squatted like fat dark mushrooms in the muted landscape.

"It's beautiful," she whispered in awe.

Chad tightened the arm that circled her waist, molding her to his side. The trailing willow limbs made a shushing sound as a warm breeze brushed them against the side of the truck.

"Come on." He pushed open his door and tugged her after him as he slid from behind the steering wheel. He led her to the front of the vehicle, then leaned back against it. Grasping her shoulders, he turned her to face the meadow, then pulled her back against his solid frame and wrapped his arms across her waist. His chin rested against her temple and his breath stirred her hair.

Megan remained rigid for several heartbeats, knowing she had to resist what was happening. Knowing she didn't want to. Finally, with a sigh, she succumbed to the symphony of tree frogs and crickets, and relaxed in the circle of Chad's embrace.

He clenched his arms, gathering her close, and dropped a kiss on her cheek. She squeezed his arms where they held her, acutely aware of the softness of Chad's lips, the warmth of his breath.

She stirred against her confinement. "Chad . . ."

"Shhh, let me hold you," he whispered, "just hold you, that's all." He hugged her tightly for a moment, as though trying to absorb her into himself. Then gently, he turned her and dropped a soft kiss on her lips.

She linked her arms around his neck and looked up into his eyes. The glow she saw there touched her heart. As he returned her gaze, his hands carefully cupped her face, then one moved up to stroke her hair.

The night sounds died under the thunder of her heartbeats. The moonlight bowed to the brilliance of shooting stars and incandescent rainbows. Megan knew she was lost.

Chad tucked her head under his chin. "Megan," he whispered, "I think I'm in love with you."

She wanted to weep with joy, she wanted to run in terror. "You . . . you can't be," she gasped. "We've just met, you can't love me!"

He tucked her face against his neck again and sighed. She felt him swallow. Twice. "I know we've just met. As for the 'can't', I'm pretty sure I do, so I guess I can."

"But Chad . . ."

"No 'but's' about it." He buried his face in her hair as he hugged her against his solid chest, and she gave up her struggle for reason.

She had no idea how long they'd stood there like that, she with her face nestled against his strong neck, he with his arms locked possessively around her, when finally he announced, "Looks like my folks are home. How about we go get a bowl of ice cream?"

Megan suffered from mood swings all day long. One moment she was on top of the world, tasting Chad's kisses, reveling in his declaration of love. The next, she plummeted earthward in spiraling panic—he *couldn't* love her, he didn't even know her. He had to be after something—it was Harry all over again.

But what if he did love her? Would he change his mind when he found out about Harry? Her head spun. And if he did love her, how did she feel about him? She stopped wiping down tables and stared at the shiny lid of the salt shaker in her hand.

Just thinking about him started her pulse racing and accelerated her breathing, but that didn't mean she loved him. You just didn't fall in love in less than a week!

"Miss, I'm ready for my check now."

She glanced over at the elderly rancher who'd addressed her. "It's under the edge of your plate, Mr. Hertz," she reminded him gently. After she'd taken his dinner order twice—for two different entrees—Celia took her aside and explained that, while in possession of all his other faculties, Mr. Hertz was notoriously absent-minded.

Resuming her task with vigor, Megan polished the tables briskly, telling herself her increased heart rate was a result of the physical labor, not thoughts of Chad.

"You don't listen too good, do you?"

Megan straightened to face Nadine. "What now?"

"I told you to stay away from Chad."

"Nadine," Megan said with strained patience, "I don't go looking for him, he comes to me. What's your problem, anyway?"

"I don't have a problem, but you will if you don't keep your distance."

Megan watched the other woman stalk off, none of the usual sultry sway in her movements. "Must be a case of unrequited love," she murmured to herself.

"You working tonight, Meg?"

She glanced at Celia, polishing the adjoining table. "No, I'm on the early shift today."

"Gonna see Chad?"

Megan tried to keep her voice flat and matter-of-fact. "Hadn't planned on it. I'll probably do laundry, maybe read a little."

Celia gave a noncommittal grunt and moved on to the next table.

" 'Scuse me, ma'am?"

Megan started as her gaze flew from the pages of her book to the immense figure looming over her. The churning washing machines had covered the sound of his approach. In one swift glance she took in his enormous size and menacing appearance. The man had to be nearly seven feet tall. Large tattoos covered his beefy arms from wrists to the ragged armholes of his smelly grease-stained shirt. A heavy beard obscured most of his face. Shaggy hair hung in lank strands to his shoulders. A leather thong circled his thick neck and a dangling silver earring flashed from under his unkempt hair.

Her pulse rate picked up and fear lodged in her throat. She threw a panicked glance at the door on the far side of the laundry room. The behemoth stood between her and the only exit. No one would hear her cries from here.

"Sorry, didn't mean to startle you," the bear-like man rumbled.

"Tha . . . ," Megan cleared her throat, trying to disguise her fear and tried again, "that's okay."

He nodded his shaggy head once, firmly. "I was hopin' you could help me."

"Me?" she squeaked.

"Yeah." Holding his hands palm out, he indicated himself. "Had to work on my rig by the side of the road. Billie usually takes care of this stuff, but she's not with me this trip."

The tide of fear ebbed slightly and Megan cocked her head at the driver. "You . . . you want me to wash your clothes?"

The fearsome features dissolved in a grin. "Shoot, no. She'd never let me hear the end of it. Just tell me how to get this mess out."

She studied him warily for a moment. It was probably safer to play along. "I'm not sure anything will get it all, but try this degreaser." She handed him a bottle from her laundry basket. "You'll probably have to run those things through a couple of cycles at least, but this should get most of it."

"Thanks. Like I said, when Billie's with me, she does it . . ."

"But she couldn't make it this trip," Megan finished and offered a tremulous smile.

The bear grinned wider than ever. "That's right. She just had a baby, our first." He reached for his back pocket.

"And you just happen to have a picture?" she guessed, her fear rapidly dissolving.

"One or two." He chuckled and handed her a packet of two dozen snapshots, then took the seat next to her. "Pardon my manners, name's Booth, Booth Harris."

"A pleasure to meet you. I'm Meg."

"You a driver?"

"No, I'm working in the cafe for Eileen."

"Fine lady, Miz Eileen."

"Yes, she is."

The formalities over, he stabbed a grimy, blunt finger at the top picture, one showing a petite brunette cuddling a newborn. "That's Billie and our Amy Jo. 'Bout four hours old there." He took the picture from her hand. "This next one's better, you can tell more what she looks like."

Megan smiled to herself. This fearsome-looking man was nothing more than the proverbial gentle giant, and a proud new papa to boot.

She'd just closed the dryer door on her load when Booth reappeared, freshly scrubbed, a laundry bag under his arm. Taking in his gleaming shoulder-length hair, now neatly combed, and fresh jeans, she teased, "Hey, you clean up pretty good."

Spots of color tinted his cheeks above the groomed beard as he returned her smile. "That's what Billie always says."

"I can tell you miss her."

"Yeah, but I'll be home tonight."

"Oh, you're not staying over?"

"Naw, just stopped to eat and get cleaned up. With a new baby, she don't need me haulin' home dirty clothes and trackin' grease through the house."

"I suppose not. Do you have much farther to go?"

"Only five hours after I leave here. Should get home about midnight."

"There you are."

They both turned to the voice in the doorway and Booth rumbled, "Chad, how ya doin'?"

"Just fine, Booth. How about you?"

"Great, Billie had the baby last week."

"Congratulations, boy or girl?"

"Girl."

Chad's gaze had rested on Megan during most of the exchange, his eyes communicating with her on a wholly different level than his conversation with Booth. Heat climbed her neck as her pulse kicked up a notch.

"Ah," she cleared her throat, wanting to break the spell he was weaving with just his look. "Booth has pictures. Show him Amy Jo's pictures. I'll start your laundry."

"Naw, I'll do the wash, you show Chad the pictures," and he handed her the precious packet.

She spread the photographs out on the lid of a washer and Chad stepped close, trapping her by bracing a hand on the machine. He appeared to concentrate as she told him about each snapshot, but his face was nearer than necessary to hers, and his breath teased her cheek.

Finally, she murmured, "Chad, stop it."

"I can't," he whispered.

"What do you mean, you can't?"

"I can't stop loving you."

"You don't love me," she bit out under her breath.

"Do too."

"Do *not*," she gritted, then slid from the cage formed by his body and arm and stomped out.

Booth's curious glance swung from Meg's departing back to Chad, who grinned and declared, "The woman's crazy about me," before taking off after her.

He caught up with her just as she reached the mini-mart door, no doubt headed for her room. Grabbing her hand, he stopped her flight. "Megan, come on. What are you peeved about?"

She bit her lips and didn't answer.

"Look at me." He lifted her chin with a gentle nudge. "What did I do? Is it something I said?"

"You know what you said."

"What? What did I say wrong? The only thing I've had a *chance* to say to you this evening is 'there you are' and . . ."

"And?"

"And that I love you. Why should that upset you?"

"You don't love me, so stop saying it. You haven't known me long enough to love me."

He brushed a finger down the side of her face. "Why don't you want me to be in love with you?"

"You are *not* . . ."

"We need to talk," he interrupted. "Let's go to your room."

"In your dreams!"

"Yeah," he muttered, "waking and sleeping. Okay, how about my truck. We'll just sit in the truck in the middle of a public parking lot, how about that?"

"I don't know what we have to talk about," she grumbled as he towed her along behind him.

"Don't worry about it, I do. Come on."

He opened the passenger door and stepped back

with exaggerated politeness, gesturing her in with a sweep of his arm. Slamming the door behind her, he marched around to the driver's side, climbed in, slammed his door, checked it, then leaned back, giving her as much room as possible.

"Now, listen and listen good," he growled. "I am nearly thirty years old, I think I should know whether or not I'm in love."

She opened her mouth but he forestalled her with a raised hand. "And I am! Now, I'm not sure how it happened, or why you don't like the idea, but that doesn't change the fact."

Her gaze dropped to where her hands twisted in her lap and he softened his tone. "Why do you object, Megan? I know I'm not handsome or rich, or anything like that, but I can tell when I kiss you that you're not exactly repelled."

Her face heated and Megan gave a choked little laugh. "Not exactly," she agreed.

"So what is it?"

She just shook her head and continued to stare at her hands.

Chad tossed his hat on the dashboard and ran his fingers through his hair in exasperation. He sighed and leaned his head back against the door frame, studying her silent profile. "Does it have anything to do with your running away to Texas?" he asked quietly.

Her head snapped up and startled brown eyes gave him his answer. "What . . . how did . . ."

"Tell me about it?"

"No! I . . . I mean there's nothing to tell."

"What are you running from, Megan?"

"I'm not running from anything, you don't know what you're talking about!"

"I'm talking about what would make an intelligent woman leave her job and home, pack only the barest necessities in a worn-down little car and drive as far as her money would carry her."

He reached over and laid a hand on the back of her neck. "Since you're trying to avoid getting involved with me, I'd guess the 'what' is a man." His voice dropped to become softer, gentler. "Now for the 'who'. A boyfriend? A husband?"

She crossed her arms defensively and stared out her window, her faced turned away from him. "I don't want to talk about it."

"But I'm right?" he prodded quietly.

She nodded.

"Do you still love him?"

She dropped her gaze to her lap and gave him only the slightest shake of her head.

A wave of relief washed over him with the power of a tidal wave, lifting his heart and his spirits on its crest. He gave her neck an affectionate squeeze. "Okay. Want to go for a drive, maybe get a drink somewhere?"

She shook her head.

"A Coke?" he prodded. "A milkshake?"

A reluctant smile lifted one corner of her mouth but she continued to shake her head. "Nothing, thanks."

"Well, I don't particularly want to go sit in the cafe where everyone will watch us like hawks."

"No," she agreed and reached for the door handle. "I need to finish my laundry. The dryer should be about done."

"I want to spend some time with you, Megan."

"You just did, see you later." She slipped from the truck and was gone.

Chad cursed in frustration, but knew it wouldn't be wise to push her any more tonight. He started the engine and headed home. He'd hit the nail on the head, and she'd admitted it. She'd left Kansas to get away from a man, but who? Why? She didn't wear a wedding ring and there was no sign she ever had, so he didn't think there'd be a husband tracking her down. That left a boyfriend.

He had the who, now he just needed to figure out the why. The why that made her so leery of him. Had she been abused emotionally or maybe even physically? The thought of any man raising a hand to her knotted the tendons in his wrists and forearms in protest, bringing his attention to the white-knuckled grip he had on the steering wheel. Forcing himself to relax, he realized he'd probably try to kill the son of a gun if that were the case and he ever met up with the guy.

From her secluded vantage point, Megan watched him go, her heart tapping out a rapid little tune. *Not handsome or anything, my Aunt Fanny! Chad Winslow is the best looking man I've ever laid eyes on, let alone kissed. And he's so sweet. Even when he's annoyed.* With a sigh she turned back to the laundry room.

She supposed she did owe him an explanation, but he hadn't pushed, and she loved him for that. No! No, she *appreciated* him for that, *appreciated* is the word she wanted.

Two washing machines churned, presumably working on Booth's clothes. He must have gone to eat. She picked up the book she'd abandoned, but her eyes didn't see the page before her.

Is it really possible to fall in love so quickly? I can't deny there's an attraction there. Megan snorted to herself. *Attraction? There's an understatement for you. The air fairly crackles when he's around, I keep waiting for the lightning bolts! But isn't love more than that? You need caring, respect, common interests.*

She had to admit Chad was a very caring individual. Look at the way he'd stopped to help her, the way he'd fixed her car. And he was an honorable man. She'd never seen him treat anyone as less than an equal, from Jamie's little brother, Carlos, to absentminded old Mr. Hertz.

Chad patiently answered the child's questions as seriously as though conversing with another adult, and laughed at Mr. Hertz's jokes as heartily on the third telling as on the first. And other than wanting to touch her whenever possible, he respected her wishes when told to back off.

But what about common interests? There it was. She didn't know enough about him to know if they shared any, other than the heat they generated when together. You *can't* love a man after just a few hours together.

But that, she finally decided, didn't mean she couldn't invest a few more hours in making his acquaintance. Though once bitten, twice shy, had her doubting him, she couldn't shake the feeling that fate might being playing a role here. She owed it to herself to investigate the possibility.

That decision made, she leaned her head back against the wall and watched her clothes going around in the dryer while her mind replayed scenes of time spent with Chad.

Chapter Six

A towel wrapped around her body, Megan perched on the toilet, shaving her legs. "Drat," she muttered when an unexpected rap on the door made her nick herself. She grabbed a piece of tissue to press against the small wound and called out, "Just a minute."

A check through the peep-hole revealed Chad standing with his hat balanced on an upturned palm in a parody of a turn-of-the-century tintype. However, instead of the somber expression customary in photographs of that era, his teeth were bared in a ridiculous grin. Smiling to herself, she demanded in feigned annoyance, "What do *you* want?"

"Can Megan come out and play?"

She stifled a giggle. "No, she most certainly cannot!"

"Why not?" he cajoled.

"She just got out of the shower."

"Oh? Well, I've got something I want to show her."

"Yeah, right," she answered in a voice heavy with sarcasm.

"No, seriously. You don't want to spend your day off in your room, do you?"

"Who said I planned to?"

"Would you open the door, I hate having to talk through it."

"No can do, I told you . . ."

"Oh, you mean you *literally* just got out of the shower?"

"Yes."

"That's okay, I don't mind."

She laughed out loud. "Go away!"

"Do you really have plans for today?"

"No."

"Then would you spend it with me?"

She hesitated as though thinking it over then answered, falsely reluctant, "Oh, all right. Give me fifteen minutes then order me up coffee, scrambled eggs and bacon. I'll be there in half an hour."

"You got it."

He walked away whistling and she felt like doing the same. Twenty minutes later she checked her reflection in the mirror, giving her hair a final fluff. The animated face that gazed back came as a bit of a surprise. Sparkling eyes and a soft smile radiated in a complexion flushed with excitement. She almost didn't recognize herself. That, more than anything else, brought home just how much Harry had taken from her—and what Chad was giving her back.

With a replete sigh, Megan laid her fork on the empty plate, and Chad grinned. "You sure can put it away," he teased, "I know ranch hands who don't eat that much."

"In your ear, cowboy," she sniffed, then stole the last slice of bacon from his plate.

"Leave the girl alone," Celia admonished as she re-filled their coffee cups. "A healthy appetite shows a great appreciation for life."

Chad's gaze swept Megan quickly and one corner of his mouth lifted in a wry smile. "So I've noticed," he murmured.

She shot him a disgusted look but had to fight hard to keep a pleased smile from giving her away.

Chad settled his hat on his head. "How do you feel about horses?"

"I love them, but they scare me a little."

"You don't ride, then?"

"Not really." Disappointment flashed across his face and she quickly added, "But if you're offering to teach me, I'd like to learn."

You'd think she'd just handed him the moon. The most beautiful smile she'd ever seen lighted his handsome features, adding an extra sparkle to his deep blue eyes. There was no helping herself, she had to smile in return.

He stood and reached for her hand, pulling her to her feet. "I can't think of anything I'd like better," he vowed, then amended, "well, I can, but . . ."

Megan snatched her hand back and he chuckled. "Come on, let's go make a cowgirl out of you." He slipped his hand to the back of her neck and headed them both out the door.

"Do you have any boots, something with a heel?" he asked, glancing at her tennis shoes as they crossed the parking lot. "And a hat?"

"Not real riding boots, but I have something I think will work, I'll be right back."

She hurried to her room to change, leaving Chad to speak with his father. Minutes later she returned wearing short-topped fashion boots with a western-styled heel, a baseball cap perched square on her head and her hair pulled back in a ponytail.

She stuck one foot out for inspection. "Will these do?"

Chad's gaze took in the boot, then traveled quickly up the length of her all the way to the cap on her head. "Looks just fine to me," he drawled, "just fine."

Heat again shot up her face and she arched an aggravated brow at him. "On second thought . . ." she began, but he grabbed her hand before she could change her mind. Laughing, he dragged her behind him out the door. "Come on Calamity Jane, it's too late to chicken out now, I've got a horse with your name on it."

Once in the truck, Chad looked over to where she

sat next to the door and wordlessly patted the seat beside him. She didn't alter her cool expression, but merely flicked a glance in his direction before complying with his request. She settled close to his side and for the second time that morning, battled the pleased little smile that begged to escape.

He swung the truck out of the parking lot and onto the roadway. "So you've never ridden before?"

"Oh, sure, but only docile riding-stable type stuff. You know, the bridle trails at the park, where the horses have been there for years and never go above a walk and all you have to do is not fall off."

"That's a start." He flashed her an encouraging grin.

"Yeah, right. That's as close to real riding as driving my Ford on the highway is to Indy racing."

"Well, at least you're smart enough to realize it," he teased.

She dropped her gaze to her lap. "I'm not stupid, Chad," she whispered, "not usually, anyway."

"Hey," he grabbed for her hand, his voice heavy with concern, "I know that, babe, I'm only teasing."

"I know." She avoided his eyes and they made the rest of the drive in silence.

"Here we are," he announced unnecessarily when they pulled up by the barns. He held her hand as he slid out of his seat, then steadied her as she slid out behind him. When she alighted, he raised her knuckles to his lips for a quick kiss, then jerked his head in the direction of the nearest barn. "Let's go meet Maybelle."

Megan soon found herself nose to muzzle with a small reddish-brown mare, hoping that the large dark eyes were regarding her with benevolence. Chad scratched the white blaze that ran down the animal's face. "You're making her nervous, pet her," he instructed.

At the movement of her hand, the mare raised its head and plopped its nose in her palm, working its lips against her skin. Megan squealed and jumped back, startling the horse into doing the same.

Chad broke out laughing. "I don't know about you girls," he chuckled. "But it looks to me like you're two of a kind."

"I thought she was going to bite me," Megan grouched.

"And she thought you were going to give her some sugar," he countered. He reached for a small tin sitting nearby and withdrew a couple of sugar cubes. "Here." He handed them to her and showed her how to offer them on her flattened palm.

"Now don't squeal and jump like that again, you'll make a nervous wreck out of the poor thing," he admonished.

"Make *her* a nervous wreck," Megan muttered and held back, glaring at him.

"Come on," he coaxed, "she's really very gentle. Her whiskers will tickle, but she's not going to bite you. She'll pick the sugar up with her lips, not her teeth."

"You're sure?"

"I'm sure." His blue eyes held a wealth of meaning as he added softly, "Trust me."

Megan swallowed and nodded, then took a step towards Maybelle's stall and raised her hand in a slow smooth movement. The mare eyed her for a moment before deciding to accept the peace offering.

Just before the animal lowered its head, Chad's hand stole to the back of Megan's neck, lending her encouragement. At that moment, deep in her heart, trust was born with the sure knowledge that this man *would* protect her. He'd stand by her and would never set her up to be hurt.

The sugar consumed, Maybelle snuffled in Megan's empty palm then butted her massive forehead against the outstretched hand seeking a scratching like a cat or dog might.

"Oh, there's a pretty girl," Megan cooed, releasing the breath she'd been holding as she scratched the mare between the eyes. "Yes, you're a fine one, aren't you?"

Chad squeezed her neck gently in approval. "Now you're getting the hang of it. Some sweets and a little flattery go a long way."

Megan shot him a look over her shoulder. "You *are* talking about horses, aren't you?"

His teeth flashed in a mischievous grin. "At the moment."

Fat white dumpling clouds gleamed against an impossibly blue sky. The first tentative incursion of autumn had broken summer's relentless hold this morning, giving the air a touch of softening. The slight breeze held just a promise of the cooler weather to come, dropping the temperature to a more comfortable eighty-two. Megan glanced over at Chad and sighed her contentment.

"You okay?" he asked.

They'd ridden up to the willow tree by the pond and he sat astride his black gelding with an ease she admired.

"Fine so far." She tipped her head back and inhaled the sweet air. "It's such a beautiful day, isn't it?"

"Yeah," he croaked, then cleared his throat, "beautiful."

"Where to now?"

He nodded to his right. "We'll walk them down to that meadow, then we'll try picking up the pace a little. It's pretty flat there so you shouldn't have any trouble, but if you do happen to fall off, the thick grass will soften the impact."

"Fall off? Chad, I really don't think I want to do this."

"Relax, you're doing great. Maybelle is beginning to trust you."

Megan muttered, "Thanks a lot," but actually felt more confident than she had a short while ago.

In no time at all she'd found her seat and was loping across the grassy expanse at Chad's side, laughing for the simple pleasure of it. A couple of calves bucked and took off in the other direction, spurred into a game of chase. A hawk circled high above them, then dove to earth and away again.

After several minutes, Chad drew his mount back to a slower pace and nodded to an oak tree. "Let's take a break, we don't want to wear you out all at once."

"I'm not tired."

"Maybe not, but selected parts of your anatomy are going to know you've taken up riding, so if you want to be able to crawl out of bed in the morning, you'll take my advice."

"You sound like an old geezer," Megan complained.

"Not old, *experienced*."

She smiled at his jest, but a small bit of the light seemed to go out of the day. She had little doubt he was experienced in more areas than just horsemanship, and it bothered her to think that other women had shared his life.

They dismounted and he took her hand, leading her to the base of the spreading tree. They sat in its shade and Chad leaned against the trunk, his arm around her shoulders, tucking her against his side. She tipped her head back and looked up through the canopy of branches and leaves, listening to the breeze that played there. A melancholy sigh joined the sound.

His wide hand stroked her arm. "What's the matter?" he asked.

"Nothing. It feels good to unwind."

His face nuzzled her hair. "Um-hmm."

"Chad?"

"Humm?"

"Are you seeing someone?"

He stiffened for a split second before squeezing her shoulders and lowering his lips to her ear. "I'm seeing you."

"No, I mean before I showed up."

"Not for quite awhile."

"How long is *quite awhile*?"

"A couple of years. Jealous?"

"That long? You're not lying to me?"

His lips caressed the skin just below her ear. "No, Megan, I'm not lying to you." He nibbled on her ear-lobe.

"You seriously expect me to believe you haven't been out with anyone in two years?"

He sighed and gave up his pleasurable excursion. "I didn't say that. I go out occasionally, but there's been no one in particular in that time."

"What happened?"

"Nothing."

She craned around to give him an exasperated glare.

"Honest, that's what happened—nothing. We enjoyed being together. A lot. We liked the same movies, the same people, the same foods, but there was never any real chemistry. Not like what you'd want to build a lifetime together on. We were more like best friends than anything."

"You're trying to tell me you went with a woman and never kissed her?"

His laugh rumbled around her. "No, we liked kissing too. But then one day she met someone new. Someone who, in her words, wasn't just fun to kiss." He chuckled wryly. "The way she explained it, kissing me gave her *warm fuzzies.* Kissing him was more a matter of life and death. They have a little boy now and are expecting another early in the spring."

"Do you still think about her?"

"Only to wish that I could find what she did. That life and death feeling." He dropped his lips to her ear and whispered, "and now I have."

"Chad . . ."

In one smooth move he repositioned her, pulling her into his arms. She had no time to react before his mouth covered hers in a sweet, melting kiss. The kiss ended and she blinked a couple of times trying to clear her thoughts. The only thing that came to mind was *a matter of life or death.*

Chad ran a roughened fingertip over her lips and murmured, "Come on, let's get you back on that horse before you stiffen up too much to climb into the saddle."

Back at the barn, they unsaddled the animals and Chad taught her how to curry her mount before putting it away. "Here." He extended a tin pail. "Give them a little treat after a ride and they'll be happy to see you next time."

"You're kidding me, right?"

He shook his head and laughed. "You've got to be the most suspicious woman I've ever known. No, I'm not kidding you. Horses are very intelligent animals.

I'd bet that after only one more outing, Maybelle would know the sound of your walk the next time you entered the barn."

"Really?"

"Sure. Provided you didn't wait several weeks, of course. If she got to know you on a daily basis, you could be gone much longer though and she wouldn't forget."

Megan offered the oats to the mare, cooing endearments as she rubbed the long neck.

"How about you?" he asked. "You've put in a good morning, are you ready for a snack?"

Sliding him a look out of the corner of her eye, Megan mused tauntingly, "Compliments and sweets?"

"What?" Then he realized what she'd said and grinned evilly. "Whatever works."

Megan smacked him in the midsection with the empty pail. He caught it with both hands as she tossed her head and strode past him to the barn door. Just as she reached the opening she yelled back over her shoulder, "Last one to the house does the dishes," and took off running.

She heard the clatter of metal hitting the dirt yard and ran for all she was worth, but as she reached the bottom step, his large form hurtled them and landed on the porch ahead of her. "No fair," she protested.

Breathless but triumphant, Chad smiled down at her. "Oh yes it is. You had a head start *and* the advantage of knowing there was going to be a race." He held the screen door open. "It was your idea, so be a good loser."

Chad directed her to the bathroom to wash up, and used the kitchen sink for himself. He'd poured them each a big glass of tea and was setting out sandwich fixings when she rejoined him.

Her spiky eyelashes and fresh pink completion attested to the fact that she'd splashed her face liberally with cool water. The cap was gone and her hair brushed smooth again, the ponytail bouncing as she crossed the kitchen to stand beside him.

He caught her hand and pulled her closer, then dragged the elastic band from her hair and fluffed the freed skeins around her shoulders. She submitted quietly to his ministrations and he dropped a kiss on the end of her nose when he'd finished. Then he led her to the kitchen counter. With a sweep of his hand he indicated the cold cuts, condiments, and breads. "Everything you need to build a hearty lunch."

What a perfect day! Megan tilted her head back and let hot water sluice the shampoo from her hair. She welcomed the heat pelting her tired muscles as it eased the tightness from her legs. Chad hadn't lied, her body was sore. She soaped the washcloth and ran it over her arms.

They'd spent the entire day together. After lunch he'd shown her the other barn where they treated cattle, the equipment sheds, explained the need for the different pens, and told her everything he could think of about raising beef. He answered all her questions as if they were quite reasonable, although she suspected some must have sounded awfully dumb to him.

Then they'd gotten in the truck and driven over a good portion of the Winslow spread, stopping each time they came upon some of the hands so that Megan could be introduced to the ranch cowboys. That had been a surprise, almost as if he were showing her off.

Chad suggested taking her out for supper and she'd agreed, saying she'd need to come back and clean up first. He changed his mind, offering instead to grill some steaks, and Meg got the feeling Chad just didn't want her out of his sight. So together they made supper, sharing the spacious farmhouse kitchen as they worked. Afterwards, he washed and she dried the dishes.

When he wrapped his long fingers around the back of her neck as he walked her to the truck, she slid her arm around his waist. It had felt so natural walking like that, his touch reassuring, her body close to his in the warm evening. And his goodnight kiss! Megan sighed in contentment and reached to turn off the water.

She had her answer. You really could fall in love with someone you'd known only a few days.

Chad toweled himself dry, rubbing vigorously. He felt good. Better than good, he felt great! Megan's resistance had slipped several notches today. She'd had fun, enjoyed his company, and relaxed her guard.

He knotted the towel around his waist and picked up his comb, but when he turned to the mirror his gaze was met by some fool with a silly grin on his face. "Yeah, I know," he said to the reflection, "she's sure something, isn't she?"

Nadine cornered her back by the kitchen when Megan took a breather after the midday rush. "I hear you and Chad had a cozy little time of it yesterday. I told you to stay away from him!"

Megan sighed. She'd had about all of this nonsense she could take. Dropping her voice to a snarl very like the other woman's, she replied, "I can't see that what I do, or don't do with Chad Winslow is any of your business, Nadine, so lay off!"

"Oh don't you?" came the cool reply. "Is running around with married men the thing to do where you come from?"

Megan blinked in surprise. How could the other woman know about Harry? "What?"

Nadine wore a nasty smile. "Chad *is* married, you know!"

"Chad?" Megan stumbled back a step.

"Yes, Chad," Nadine hissed.

"No . . . you're mistaken . . ." A roaring sound began to build in her head.

"Ask him," Nadine spat in disgust. "I could hardly be mistaken about something like that."

"How do you know?" Megan's mind whirled.

"What makes you so sure?" Her chest tightened, choking off her air. She fought for breath.

"I was there."

Megan swallowed. Blood pounded in her ears, her head swam. She felt dizzy, nauseated. The smug look on Nadine's face warned her, but she had to hear it, had to know for certain. Her voice a hoarse rasp, she asked, "You were there?"

"Chad is mine, you stupid little witch, and I'm not letting him go," Nadine snarled softly, her voice as ugly as anything Megan could ever have imagined. "He is *my* husband and I intend for him to stay that way, so if I even think you've been near him again, I'll tear you into little tiny pieces!"

A strangled cry of horror that had nothing to do with Nadine's threat bubbled from Megan's throat. She fell back another step, bumping a table and sending a glass smashing to the floor. The room began to whirl around her and darkness seeped in at the edges of her vision. Her heart rose up in her chest, swelling to twice its size, its pounding drowning out all other sound, before—with excruciating pain—it tore itself in two. Megan clamped a trembling hand to her mouth to stifle the cry of agony. Wresting her gaze from the satisfied glitter in Nadine's eyes, she turned and ran for the kitchen.

Hand outstretched, she shoved through the swinging doors and nearly collided with Celia. Tears blinded her and she stumbled as she went, dodging people and objects, stoves and equipment. As she pushed through the back door, she heard Alma's call, but kept on running.

Chapter Seven

Reaching her room, Megan fumbled with her keys, dropping them twice as she struggled with the lock. The door swung open and she lurched through it, slamming and bolting it behind her before she threw herself on the bed. There, she gathered the pillows in a wad to muffle her body-wracking sobs.

She'd done it again, oh God, she'd done it again! What was wrong with her, how could this keep happening?

Oh, no! Please, no! She clutched one of the pillows hard against her stomach and wept her heart out.

Someone tapped on the door. She buried her face in the other pillow and held her breath.

"Meg, it's Alma, open up. You've got to listen to me, child, it's not what you think. Open up."

94

Megan lay very still, hiccupping softly as Alma knocked several more times before finally giving up. Drawing a deep breath, she sat up and wiped her eyes with the heels of her hands. She didn't have time for any more of this, she had to get out. Now.

No way would another man play Megan Stallings for a fool! Scooting off the bed, she dragged out her suitcases and quickly tossed her clothing in. She had to leave before anyone else came looking for her. And they would. Once they found out she knew about Chad's marriage, his mother, father, aunts, cousins, and even Chad himself would come around offering explanations and excuses.

She leaned her weight on one case to compress the jumbled heap of clothing. *Well, they just won't find me.* It didn't matter why he'd done it. It didn't even matter that he might really love her. He was someone else's husband, *Nadine's* husband, and that effectively removed him from a place in her life, from the realm of her world . . . from the center of her universe.

The big luggage zipper caught on a shirt tail and she struggled to free it. Hurriedly, she poked the fabric back inside with her fingers, then slid the fastener home.

"What do you mean, she's gone?" Chad roared.

"Jist what I said, boy," his great-aunt Alma snapped over the phone. "Nadine spilled the beans."

"Nadine did what?" The menace in that quiet question was more dangerous-sounding than his roar.

"She told Meg you two was married," Alma replied in annoyance.

"When?"

" 'Bout two hours ago. I tried to talk to Meg, but she wouldn't open the door. Then I've been tryin' to get you . . . ," her voice trailed off on a weary note.

"I know. Thanks, Aunt Alma. Who else knows?"

"No one unless Nadine's been braggin', but I don't think so. Haven't seen her since, either. I figger she's hiding out, worried about what you'll do."

"She should be. My folks don't know?"

"Don't believe so. Figgered it's your business to tell 'em. Didn't even know fer sure if they was wise that you're sweet on the gal."

Chad sighed. "Yeah, they're wise, but thanks. I'll be there shortly."

He hung up the phone, and swore. *She can't be gone. Not now, not so soon. We were just beginning to build something. Something solid. I know it.*

He crammed his fingers into his hip pockets and exhaled a mighty sigh at the ceiling, tamping down his rising panic. His eyes closed and he whispered her name . . . and then a prayer.

Where would she go? She doesn't have much money. Oh God, I hope she doesn't head for Houston, I'll never find her there. Never find her . . .

With a muttered oath he snatched up his keys, slammed out of the house, disdained the porch steps, leaping instead to the ground, and left the drive in a spray of gravel. He had to catch up with her before she got too far. The more time that passed, the slimmer his chances of ever seeing her again, and he couldn't face that possibility.

He picked up the microphone to his citizen's band radio, identified himself and asked to break in on the common contact channel, nineteen. "Truck Stop Cowboy needing a break on one nine."

"Go ahead Cowboy, you got Gus Gus here."

"Hey, Gus Gus, good to hear you," Chad greeted the intrastate truck driver, who stopped often at The Depot. "I'm in need of some major assistance, over."

"What's your twenty?" The driver asked his location.

"Negative, I'm not down. I'm trying to locate a beaver in a battered white Ford Escort with Kansas plates, over."

"Which way's she headed?"

"Don't know, that's why the mayday. Spread the word and if anyone spots her, relay it to The Depot, over."

"Roger. What'd she do, drive off without paying? Over."

"Negatory, nothing like that. It's personal, over."

A chorus of whistles and cat calls poured through the radio as others on the channel gave their feedback. Chad shook his head. "All right you bear bait, all I can say is if you haven't already been there, your time is coming. Truck Stop Cowboy out."

The trucker known as Gus Gus chuckled into his radio. "You got that right, Cowboy. It's been almost two years now since Cinderella netted me, and I've never had it so good." A renewed round of whistles and ribald comments jammed the airwaves, to which the trucker replied with a chuckle, "You road tramps are just jealous. Gus Gus out."

Chad continued to monitor the CB as he drove to the truck stop, but no one reported seeing Megan's car.

"How'd she get past you?" he demanded of his un-happy father several minutes later. "Surely you didn't help carry her bags to the car?"

"Of course not," Buck snapped. "She must have gone while I was having supper."

Both men turned to Jamie. The youth jerked his head towards the far back corner of the store. "I spent a half hour restocking, she could have gone out carry-ing a piano and I wouldn't have paid any attention. Sorry."

"She'll be back, Chad, you'll see." Eileen patted her son's shoulder.

"I don't think so, Mom. She's running from some kind of man trouble in Kansas, so I don't think she's going to give me a second chance. I'll have to hunt her down if I'm going to get her back."

Megan locked her car, left it at the back of the econ-omy motel and headed around the building. The Ford would be out of sight, but she was not so foolish as to take a room back there. She'd gotten one as close as possible to the registration office.

She paused to scan the front parking lot before stepping from the shadows and heading for her new lodgings. In her room, she unpacked quickly, then laid out her clothes for work.

The little barbecue house wasn't going to pay her quite as much as Eileen had, but the tips should be good. As soon as she had enough money, she'd head down the road to Houston.

If she'd waited one more day, she'd have had her first paycheck from the cafe, but that was out of the question. She couldn't face Chad or his family, knowing what she did now. Besides, she owed most of it for her room and the parts to fix her car.

"I'm going to drive around a little, I don't think she's gone far. Not yet anyway."

Buck studied his son. "You don't think she went on to Houston?"

"Not yet. Except for her tip money, I doubt she's got a hundred dollars to her name."

Buck gave a long low whistle.

"Yeah," Chad grunted and pushed himself away from the counter.

"Want some company?"

"Thanks, Dad, that's okay."

"How about you, Chad," his mother asked, "are *you* okay?"

He gave her a half-smile. "Sure, why wouldn't I be? See you both later." He kissed his mother's cheek, and headed for his truck.

Lord, he was whipped! Why did he feel so tired? He backed the truck away from the buildings and turned it toward the highway. His shoulders slumped and his neck ached from the knotted muscles at its base. He hadn't worked that hard today, he shouldn't be this done in.

His gaze fell to the empty seat beside him and he had his answer. His body hadn't taken the beating, his heart had. His daily portion of sunlight, his dose of optimism, his plans for the future had all been ripped away with Megan's sudden departure, and his life-blood was flowing out the open wound.

He should have told her about Nadine, but there just hadn't been time.

Nadine.

He'd have to make sure she stayed put until the hoax could be exposed, or the papers served, which-ever the situation ultimately called for. He'd no inten-tion of spending the rest of his life trying to chase her down in order to end their marriage. Marriage! Yeah, right.

On the edge of town, he left the highway for the access road and began a methodical search of the park-ing lots of every motel in and around Huntsville. It was well past midnight before he conceded defeat and turned for home. Tomorrow he'd start checking apart-ment buildings, but he really didn't believe she had the money necessary for a lease.

His hands tightened on the steering wheel. The idea of Megan needing anything and not having the means to get it knotted his gut. Why couldn't she have waited around to talk to him? To get his side of the story? Knowing Nadine, he was certain that even though she'd revealed their status, there was a whole lot she *hadn't* told Megan. He knew she'd left out the part that would make a difference.

The next morning, he overslept by an hour, so when Chad reached the barn, he found one of the ranch hands already tending the cow he'd come to doctor.

"Jack," he greeted.

"Morning, Boss. Find her?"

Still groggy, Chad stared at the young man in confusion.

"Your girl, did you find her?" Jack clarified.

Chad wiped a hand down his face. "Word gets out fast around here."

A slow grin climbed the cowboy's cheek. "Well, when the most eligible bachelor in Walker County falls off the fence, it don't stay a secret long. Now maybe the rest of us will have a chance with the ladies."

Chad's quick bark of laughter died as another thought struck him. Had news of his marriage to Nadine spread as quickly? Evidently not.

"Jack, if you think you and Steve can manage things, I'm going into town."

"Sure thing. Let us know if there's anything we can do."

"Keep an eye out for her car. A little Escort, white, kind of beat-up, with Kansas plates."

"Will do. Want me to pass the word?"

"Yeah, thanks."

Sounds on the other side of the wall woke Megan. A shower running, doors opening and closing. She glanced at her alarm clock, rolled over, and pulled the covers up around her ears. She could sleep for three more hours if she wanted to; the barbecue restaurant didn't serve breakfast. She wondered guiltily how they were getting along without her at The Depot. She'd left them short-handed and without notice. Eileen deserved better than that.

But what about you, don't you deserve better? Better than another lying two-timer tearing out your heart? God in heaven, why are men such pigs? That isn't really what You'd intended, is it?

Weren't there any men left like her father? Married to her mother for thirty years, he still kissed her the moment he stepped in the door every evening and murmured, "I love you." Or her grandfather. Almost fifty-five years with the same woman and he was more devoted than ever.

Megan gasped. Her parents! She'd forgotten to call them the other day. They hadn't heard from her since Oklahoma. She needed to let them know she was all right, but first she had to find her way out of yet another mess.

Megan sighed and pulled the covers higher, over her head, but blue eyes crinkled at her from her memory, from beneath a lock of sable hair, falling over a tanned forehead. "Oh, Chad," she whispered.

She had to get out of Huntsville soon or run the risk of going back to him. Obviously, will power wasn't one of *her* best features. She wondered, miserably, if Catholic convents accepted Baptist girls.

Chad crossed his arms on his desk and rested his forehead on them. Lord, it'd been a long day. He'd secured Nadine's promise to be available when the papers were ready to be served by offering her a tidy sum of cash, payable upon the dissolution of their marriage. Then he'd come back to the house to spend literally hours with the classified directory and the telephone. He'd called practically every apartment complex within easy commuting distance of Huntsville, with no luck. He'd finish the list tomorrow.

Then what? If you still don't find her, then what are you, going to do? He raised his head and scrubbed his palms over his face. He didn't know what he'd do. Take out newspaper ads? Lease billboards? Offer a reward? Strangle Nadine?

Now that one sounded like a winner. It wouldn't find Megan, but it sure as heck would make him feel better!

With a weary sigh, he pushed himself from his chair and went to the kitchen for a sandwich. He reached into the refrigerator for a beer, decided that wouldn't taste the greatest with peanut butter and jelly, and got out the milk instead.

Where is she, why did she run like that? He knew why she'd left, she believed him a married man. *But why take off without a word? Wouldn't most women want to settle up first? Scream, call names, threaten murder and/or mutilation? And why leave Kansas in the first place, what was she running from there?*

Suddenly, he knew. There was no doubt in his mind whatsoever. The man she'd left behind was married. That knowledge only gave rise to more questions. Had she known it beforehand? Had he lied to her, promised to leave his wife for her?

Poor Megan, she had to be hurt and confused, no wonder she'd disappeared. *Hang on honey, I'll find you and we'll get it all cleared up.*

For the next few days Chad rose earlier than usual, getting as much work done as he could by noon. Then he'd leave it to the ranch hands and continue his search. Driving up and down the streets of Huntsville, he checked the parking lots of motels and apartment houses. He talked on his CB, asking if anyone had seen her car, requesting they keep a watch for her. He added Sam Houston State College to his route, cruising the campus in search of a little white Ford.

The third time he arrived at the school, a sheriff's deputy pulled him over. "May I see your driver's license, please."

"What's the problem, I wasn't speeding, was I?"

"I need to see your license, please, sir."

"Sure, just a second." Chad dug it out of his wallet.

The officer perused the document. "Are you a student here, Mr. Winslow?"

"No." Chad didn't know this man, he must be new to the force.

"May I ask what your business is here on campus?"

"I'm looking for a friend. Why did you stop me?"

"You've been observed cruising the school."

"Well, if you take such close note of all the traffic through here maybe you can help me. My friend drives a white Ford Escort with Kansas tags."

"Your truck is different enough to be noticed," the officer replied, flicking a quick glance over the forty-odd-year-old vehicle, "a Ford compact isn't. Sorry."

Chad tapped his fingers on the steering wheel while his name, address, and license number were copied by the officer.

"Would you mind telling me why you're looking for your friend here? Can't you call him at home?"

"It isn't a he, it's a she, and she, ah . . . she's avoiding me."

The officer looked up sharply. "And why is that?"

"We had a misunderstanding."

"I see. Would you please step out of the truck?"

Chad sighed, and slowly climbed down to stand beside—he squinted at the man's name tag—Sims, T. Sims. "I can explain everything."

"Give it a try," Sims invited. When Chad finished, he said, "Wait right where you are," and walked to his patrol car. He reached inside for the microphone, keeping his eyes on Chad.

"Talk to Duke Koeller, he knows me," Chad called out. Hopefully Duke would be around. Chad had the uneasy feeling he'd need his friend to back him up if he wasn't to spend the rest of the day answering questions. Or worse.

Chad couldn't catch Sims' end of the conversation, but he evidently made comment on his suspect's mental condition, because Duke's laugh rolled from the radio followed by, "Yeah, he's sick all right, but he's not dangerous. Poor boy's just lovesick, Sims. Do what you can to help him out."

Thanks a lot Duke, I owe you one! Chad hoped the embarrassed flush had receded by the time Sims came back.

"Sorry, Winslow, can't be too careful these days." The young officer held the license out to him.

"I understand."

Chad swung by the truck stop on his way home, needing the encouragement his family always offered. Today was better than that, his father had news.

"A driver came through about half an hour ago, thought he saw Meg's car on the other side of town, but she exited the freeway before he got close enough to check her license plate."

Armed with the street name of the exit she'd taken—he had to believe it was her—Chad jumped back into his truck. Three hours of scouring the area turned up nothing.

This just wasn't going to work. Though not actually

a big town, finding one person in Huntsville had turned into the proverbial search for the needle in a haystack. Chad hadn't been this discouraged since the moment he'd learned of her departure.

He fell into bed completely exhausted, both emotionally and physically. His last thought before drifting off into an uneasy sleep, was a promise to Megan; his talisman against the growing fear that he might not succeed. *Hang on, babe, I'll find you.*

Megan was dead on her feet. The little restaurant did a brisk business, but the restless nights took even more of a toll. She'd fall into an uneasy sleep only to dream of Chad, then awake with a pounding headache. How could she fall so hard in such a short time? What was there about that blue-eyed cowboy that could so thoroughly destroy her life? She hadn't hurt this badly over Harry and she'd known him much, much longer.

The very thought of Chad made her long for the comfort of his arms. Although he was the problem, instinctively she knew he could make it better. But at what price?

She missed the warmth of his touch, the sound of his voice so badly she physically ached from it. Just to see his smile one more time! To touch the hair at the back of his neck, to watch his eyes sparkle with laughter . . . or darken with desire just before he kissed her. A sob tore from her throat and she threw herself down on the bed to cry some more.

Drat! Now she'd need to re-do her makeup before she left for work.

Pocketing the tip, she sighed. With today's lunch crowd her nest egg was growing rapidly. Soon she'd have enough to move on. When she added this week's paycheck to the tips she'd already garnered, she'd have around two hundred and fifty dollars more than when she'd left The Depot. Another week or two and she'd have what she needed. However, if waitressing jobs were as easy to come by in Houston as she'd found them to be here, she wouldn't need much to tide her over.

"Hey, Booth, over here."

Her head snapped around as the customer seated in a corner table hailed a new arrival. *Please, let there be another man with that name.* There were probably several in the world with that name, but not here, not this afternoon.

Chapter Eight

Megan ducked into the kitchen as the burly truck driver joined his friend.

"Sue, I need a quick break, would you take my tables?"

"Sure, Meg. Are you okay?"

"I'll be fine, thanks." Ducking her head, she slipped out of the kitchen and into the women's rest room where she stayed as long as she dared. Evidently it was long enough. When she peered out, Booth and his friend were gone. "Close call," she muttered to herself as she cleared the table, leaving the tip for Sue to pick up.

She'd never thought about running into anyone who might divulge her whereabouts. She'd only been in town a few days before leaving The Depot, she didn't know many people, for goodness' sake. Besides, what difference would it make if Booth had seen her, he wouldn't know what had happened between her and Chad.

Chad. He'd probably forgotten all about her. Only in her imagination did he care. Only in her troubled dreams did he search for her. When she managed to sleep at all.

"Ahem."

Megan jumped at the discreet cough and found a couple waiting to claim the table she'd been absently wiping.

She couldn't get Chad off her mind the rest of the day. After hours spent in vain attempts at exorcising him from her conscious thoughts, he'd returned with a vengeance. Seeing Booth had been the catalyst, of course, but no matter how hard she tried, she just couldn't dislodge Chad's image this time.

She knew it wasn't only that he'd stuck in her mind, he'd burrowed into her heart as well. With an agony of spirit she castigated herself. "Fool," she whispered as she quickly swiped the tears from her eyes.

When the restaurant finally closed for the night, she barely had the energy left to drag herself to her car. Fighting Chad's memory today had added an extra burden to the drain of a physically demanding job and the nights of fitful sleep.

Disheartened, she trudged across the parking lot to where her car waited hidden behind the dumpster. She furtively scanned the shadows as she went, half expecting him to appear. She inserted her key in the door and turned it.

Suddenly, a shadow lashed out from under the car, brushing her leg before she could jump back. Megan screamed. The cat scampered past and shot off into the darkness.

"Easy, Meg," she muttered, a hand pressed to her chest in an effort to soothe her pounding heart. "You're getting paranoid."

At the motel she parked in her usual spot at the back. Still jumpy from the cat episode, she made her way to her room, key in hand, keeping to the illuminated passages. The walkways were quiet, the shadows unmoving.

She breathed a sigh of relief and leaned wearily against the door frame while she fumbled with the lock, then straightened and turned the knob. Stumbling into the room, she gave the door a feeble push behind her. It didn't click shut. When she turned to do the job properly her gaze fell to the toe of a boot protruding between door and jamb.

The door swung slowly inward. Too tired to be frightened, her second sense telling there was no reason to be anyway, Megan let her gaze travel slowly upward. Up past the boot, up a long denim-encased leg, up past slim hips and flat belly, up over wide shoulders. She paused briefly at the full, sober lips, then completed the journey to his eyes. The blue depths held no sparkle now. Dull and underscored by shadows, they looked as fatigued as she felt. Her heart did a back flip, then fell like a stone in her chest.

"Chad," she acknowledged flatly.

"Megan."

She turned away and moved to the small dresser where she dropped her purse and keys, then sat down on the end of the bed to pull off her shoes.

"May I come in?"

She looked over her shoulder to where he stood in the doorway. She should have left Huntsville at once. "Come ahead."

He closed the door and propped his hands on his hips, much as he had the first time they'd met. "You look done in," he observed quietly.

She nodded.

"Go take your shower. We can talk when you get out."

She gathered up her sleep shirt and robe without a word.

Hot water peppered her tired muscles, relaxing them and sapping what little strength remained. *He wanted to talk.* She didn't think she could form a cohesive thought, let alone a sentence. All the fight had gone out of her. She'd left too much of herself behind when she'd left Chad.

She dried off and looked in the mirror. Not a pretty sight. Sunken eyes stared back from a pale, drawn face. Not much there to stir a man's interest. Might as well get it over with, avoiding him hadn't solved anything.

She stepped from the bathroom to find he'd pulled a chair against the door and then gone to sleep in it. His head lolled to one side and his arms dangled downward. His legs stretched out before him, crossed at the ankles. A boot heel dug into the carpet was the only thing that kept him from sliding to the floor. She wanted to laugh . . . and to cry.

"Chad?"

He didn't stir.

"Chad?" she called a little louder.

His head snapped up and he rubbed his eyes. "Sorry, haven't slept much lately." He stretched. "Feel better after your shower?"

She shrugged and dropped her gaze as he rose to take her gently by the shoulders. The height of him, the breadth of him. How could she have forgotten so quickly? She'd thought it indelibly etched in her memory, on her senses, but as vivid as those images were, they paled in comparison to the real thing. To the real man standing here, smelling of crisp cotton and sunshine, spice and mown grass.

"Megan, we're both beat," he said gently. "I've been looking high and low for you since you left, and it appears you've been working yourself to death. We have a lot to talk about, but I think we'd be better off waiting until morning."

It felt so good just being near him again, his hands firm on her shoulders, but she kept her attention on the toes of his boots. If she looked in his face, at those lips, those eyes, she'd do something foolish, like throw her arms around his neck and beg him to take her back, and she couldn't do that. He was married to Nadine and no matter how strange that relationship might be, Megan would not interfere. She'd learned her lesson.

One hand lifted from her shoulder and settled under her chin, raising her face to his. "Okay?"

"Okay?" she repeated dumbly.

"We'll talk in the morning, okay?"

"Okay."

"That's my girl. Now come on, it's past your bedtime." He took her hand and led her around the side of the bed, then turned back the covers. "Get in," he directed as he sat on the chair and pulled off a boot.

"What are you doing?" she demanded, suddenly a little more alert.

"Getting ready for bed."

"You don't live here!"

He pulled off his other boot and dropped his foot to the floor. "Megan, if you think I'm giving you another chance to take off before we talk, you're crazy. Now I've hardly slept for a week and I'm dead on my feet. Sitting outside that restaurant since one-thirty this afternoon has my body tied in knots. All I want to do is stretch out and get some rest."

"Just rest?"

"Just rest," he promised.

"Since one-thirty?"

He nodded and began to unbutton his shirt.

"Booth?"

He nodded again and pulled off his socks.

"Won't someone worry about you?"

"My folks know where I am."

"They do?"

"Yes. Now get in bed."

Megan discarded her robe, revealing a long cotton sleep shirt printed all over with black and white cows. Chad glimpsed it before she slid beneath the sheet and shook his head, chuckling.

He stripped off except for his jeans, then slid in beside her. She'd turned her back to him and scooted as far away as possible, but he had other ideas.

He wrapped an arm around her waist and pulled her to the middle of the bed, into the curve of his body. "Come here, woman. I've lost too much sleep wondering where you were not to want to know for sure tonight."

That familiar feeling of homecoming she'd experienced at his first kiss suffused her again, warming that spot in the center of her being that had yawned cold and desolate since she'd left him. Wrapped in his arms, his strong body pressed against her back, his breath feathering her neck, she knew she was right where she should be. The only thing that could be better would be to turn and take him in her arms as well, and kiss him until they were both senseless. But she knew where that would lead, no matter how tired they thought they were.

And that couldn't happen. Not until they'd talked about Nadine.

* * *

Megan woke to find Chad perched on the edge of a chair. Pulling on his boots, he smiled. "Good morning, sunshine, sleep well?"

As a matter of fact she had. For the first time since leaving The Depot. She yawned and snuggled deeper into her pillow.

"None of that now," he protested. "Get packed, I'm taking you home."

"Won't your wife object?"

"Snappish little thing when you first wake up, aren't you?"

"Gee, I wonder why," she grumbled as she levered herself into a sitting position and leaned back against the headboard. She pushed her hair out of her face and looked up to find him grinning at her.

"We've got to do something about your taste in sleep wear," he teased.

"My sleep wear is none of your concern, cowboy, and I'm certain Mrs. Winslow will agree with me."

He sighed and shook his head. "You want to have it out here and now, I take it."

"Seems as good a place as any."

"I'd rather do it at the ranch."

"Why doesn't that surprise me? Sorry, but I hardly see that your home territory would be of any advantage to me."

"I wasn't thinking of it as home territory. I was simply thinking of it as a place where we could be alone to talk, without a bed quite so handy."

Meg flushed and pulled the covers up higher. "You really take the cake, you know that? I can't believe your gall!"

"Like it's a big surprise that I want you? Oh, come on, Megan, you're a big girl, you know very well what you do to me. I love you, for Pete's sake, of course I want you."

"You're married, Chad! You left that part out! The whole time you've been kissing me, telling me you loved me you've been married to . . . to Nadine!"

The bed gave as he lowered his frame to sit beside her. Megan scooted over to put a little space between them, but Chad picked up her hand and studied it for a moment before declaring, "I'm not really married."

Not *really* married? "Then why did Nadine say you were?"

"Well, we are. On paper."

"I've heard this story before," she sniffled.

"Yeah, I figured as much."

"What?"

"Never mind." Chad stood and paced across the small room, returning to stand in front of her, his head hanging low.

"Chad?"

He heaved a heavy sigh and ran both hands through his hair. "It's a really weird story."

Megan scooted up against the headboard and made herself comfortable. She wasn't leaving this room until she knew exactly what was going on.

Chad dropped to the edge of the bed, propped his

forearms on his thighs and studied the floor between his feet. Finally, he seemed to get his thoughts together.

"Nadine and I were in school together," he began. "Well, actually she was a couple of years behind me. I used to hang out with her brother, Dex. He's a pretty straight arrow, but Nadine has always been a little wild. Anyway, Dex called me a couple of months ago and said his sister had moved back from Houston. Seems she'd had a big fight with the guy she'd been seeing and was pretty upset about the whole thing. He said she needed a job and asked me to put a word in with the folks."

"And you did."

"Yeah, I did." Chad scrubbed his hands over his face and blew out a breath.

"And?" she prompted when it seemed he wouldn't go on.

"And she started dogging my trail. I couldn't turn around without her popping up, batting her eyes, grabbing my arm, stuff like that."

"She found a new focus in life, huh?"

An unmistakable flush climbed Chad's bronzed cheeks. "Yeah, well, she did say something along those lines once."

"And?"

"I've told you, I wasn't interested. I told her, too."

Megan scooted higher in the bed, intrigued. "Then why does she think you're married?"

"Because we might be."

"I see."

"I'm sure glad someone does," he replied in exasperated tones, "because if you do, you're the only one."

He pushed to his feet and prowled the small room. "A couple of weeks back Dex and some of the old group got together at an ice house down the road. Nadine showed up and joined in. We were drinking beer, shooting pool, some of the guys were dancing with their girlfriends, you know, that sort of thing."

He glanced at her then, and Megan rotated her hand in a get-on-with-it gesture.

"It was getting late and I was ready to call it a night, but Nadine wanted me to shoot a game with her. I begged off, but she wouldn't let it go. She was getting wound up so rather than have her spoil everyone's fun with one of her scenes, I agreed. She turned sweet as pie and went and got me a beer. I'm not sure what happened. It tasted fine, but the beer must have been contaminated or something. I started feeling really strange."

He paused and shot her a look. "And no, I wasn't drunk. I'd only had a couple of bottles the whole evening."

Megan pulled her knees up and propped her arms on them. "What do you mean by strange? Were you dizzy or sick to your stomach?"

"A little of both. My head started pounding and my stomach cramping. Nadine said something about taking me home and the next thing I knew a couple of guys were loading me into her car. Everything after that is pretty much a blur. I woke up in a motel around noon the next day, with Nadine beside me and a marriage certificate on the night table."

Megan dropped her forehead to her crossed arms. "Then you *are* married."

"I don't know!" Chad slapped the bathroom doorframe, then swung to face her. "But I *do* know one thing. I know as sure as I'm standing here that I've never laid a finger on that woman!"

"And how do you know that?" Megan cried.

"I don't know *how* I know, just that deep down inside there's a part of me that says it never happened. Nadine doesn't have a claim in this world on me."

A shiver of apprehension skittered up Megan's spine. "Do you think she drugged you?"

He pointed a finger at her nose. "Bullseye!"

"But who would perform a marriage ceremony with an unconscious groom?"

"I don't think I was unconscious, just out of my mind."

"You'd have to be to marry Nadine," Megan snapped.

A wry grin flitted across Chad's face. "You got that right."

Megan threw her arms up and plopped back against the headboard. "I don't know. This whole thing is just too wild. Nadine says you're married and threatens me if I get too close, but at the same time flirts with every man within reach. *You* say you're not *really* married, but have the document that proves it. My life is a big enough mess without this, Chad. I don't need it, I truly don't."

He'd circled the bed while she was talking and sat down beside her. Taking her hands, he folded them between his palms and said with certainty, "But you need *me*, Megan. And I need you. Please, come home. At least stay at The Depot while we get this worked out."

"Worked out? What worked out?" She tugged her hands free. "You're married, Chad!"

"I don't think so. My lawyer and an investigator are looking into it. The justice of the peace who signed the certificate is out of town. Seems he left on vacation that next day. Until we track him down, we don't know for sure that the certificate isn't a forgery."

Megan sighed and pleated the edge of the sheet between her fingers. "And if it isn't?"

"Then I get an annulment. Now come on, pack your stuff."

"What about my job?"

"You can keep it if you want, or if he needs notice, give it. It's more than you did for Mom."

"I'm sorry about that."

"It's okay. She was just glad to know I'd found you safe and sound." He dug a key out of his jeans pocket and handed it to her. "They kept your room for you."

Even with a good night's sleep, she wasn't strong enough to resist him, but she had to give it one more try. "What about Nadine? I won't be responsible for breaking up another marriage."

"It's not a marriage," he said with obvious exasperation, "and Nadine is taken care of. I'm giving her two very good job leads and enough money to set her up in an apartment in Austin. According to her, she's always wanted to live there."

"If you don't have any obligation to her, why would you give her so much?"

"Because I want to be sure she doesn't take off before my legal situation is cleared up," he shot back, then his voice softened. "I want to be free to marry you as soon as possible."

Her startled gaze met his. Blue eyes held brown and, for a moment, the troubles of the world spun away. She drew a shaky breath. He raised her hands to his lips, kissing each in turn, and her heart went wild. It skittered around in her chest like a drunken butterfly and interfered with her breathing. She must be lightheaded from the lack of oxygen, he couldn't have said what she thought he had.

"Megan," he whispered, "will you marry me?"

"Now what?" Buck asked as Chad returned from carrying the last of Megan's belongings to her room. "Do I need to rent a tux?"

Chad pushed back his hat and frowned. "Not just yet. She says she can't marry me."

"Oh? Sorry son, I could have sworn she was interested."

"I'm sure of it, but she needs more time."

Buck grunted. "So what you gonna do?"

"Give it to her, I guess. I don't have much choice."

"What about Nadine?"

"She's out of here as soon as this mess is cleared up."

"Just like that?"

"I made her an offer she couldn't refuse. I'm helping her get an apartment in Austin."

Buck raised his eyebrows in question. "You aren't going to prosecute?"

"Prosecute?"

"You suspect you were slipped a mickey, or else the certificate is forged. Either one of those is a crime."

"I can't prove I was drugged this long after the fact. And even if she forged the marriage certificate, I just want her out of my life." Chad ran a hand over his face. "Nadine is one very strange woman, but she's Dex's sister. I don't want to be responsible for adding to his worries."

Buck nodded his head sagely and snagged the ringing telephone. "It's for you." He extended the receiver to his son.

"Hello?"

"Chad, this is Duke, have you found that girl yet? The one from Kansas?"

"Yeah, thanks. Just brought her home."

"Well, that's good news. Now for the bad."

Chad felt a quick tightening in his chest. Duke hesitated, so he prompted, "Go ahead."

"The law is looking for her back home, buddy. Got a notice this morning to be on the lookout."

Chad expelled the breath he'd been holding. Somehow he'd almost expected something like this. "Did they say what they want with her?"

"Material witness to embezzlement."

"Embezzlement?"

"That's what they said."

Remembering how little she'd arrived with, Chad shook his head. "I don't believe it."

"They didn't say she was a suspect."

"Okay, Duke, thanks. I'll tell her."

"Uh, Chad? You'll need to do more than that. She has to come in and talk to us."

"Okay."

"I mean it, Chad."

"I know. What'd you think, I'll take off with her for the border?"

Duke laughed. "That wouldn't be your usual style, but who can tell with a man in love?"

"Thanks a lot, *buddy*."

"As soon as you can, okay?"

"Be there in an hour."

Chapter Nine

They'd stopped for a red light and Chad looked over at Megan. Huddled at the far end of the seat from him, arms crossed tightly over her waist and lips tucked between her teeth, she looked as if she might burst into tears at any moment. It didn't take a genius to see she was scared to death.

"Come here, you," he growled tenderly.

She didn't answer or resist as he brought her against his side. The light changed and he shifted gears, then wrapped his arm around her shoulders, holding her close. He dropped a kiss on her temple and gave her a quick squeeze before he had to withdraw his arm to again shift gears at the next intersection.

She wrapped her fingers around his biceps and scooted closer, hugging his arm against her. He

125

glanced down, but her eyes remained focused straight ahead. Her lips, however, trembled slightly. He gave her a reassuring pat. "Honey, it'll be okay. They just want to talk to you."

Megan nodded mutely and laced her fingers with his. Right now Chad was her only strength and she needed as much physical contact with him as she could possibly get. The heat of his arm against her side, the power of its muscle under her quivering fingertips, the solid weight of the wide hand resting on her leg, these were the things she concentrated on. He wouldn't let anything happen to her, she knew he wouldn't. But would she have him once this was over? Panic rose to choke her and tears brimmed on her lashes.

The officer Chad had introduced as Duke loaded a cassette into the tape recorder and glanced at Megan. "They didn't give me any background, but I expect they'll still want to talk to you, even with this taped statement."

"Will I have to go back to Kansas City?"

"I don't know, ma'am." He snapped the lid closed on the tape and glanced at Chad. "Would you mind waiting outside?"

"Yes, as a matter of fact I would."

Duke raised his eyebrows at the challenge in Chad's voice, but merely replied, "It's the lady's call."

"Please, let him stay." She locked her hands together on the table in front of her. "This way I won't have to go through it twice."

"Fine by me." Duke pulled out a chair and motioned Chad to another. "Now," he continued, "state your full name and address, then tell us in your own words everything you know about Harry Thomas."

"Everything?"

Duke nodded. "Everything . . . business and personal."

She swallowed and glanced up at Chad. *Here goes nothing.* He gave her a reassuring smile and squeezed the hand he'd taken when he sat down. She focused her gaze on their interlaced fingers and began with the day she'd first gone to work for Harry.

Chad's clasp remained firm and warm even as she chronicled her infatuation with her boss. She hastened to add that she truly believed the Thomases were estranged, but realized how naive it sounded. Chad couldn't possibly believe that.

His grip tightened when she got to the part about giving Harry all the money she had, including the proceeds from the sale of her home. *He must think I'm such an idiot!* She closed her eyes and drew a deep breath. *Well why shouldn't he? I am.*

"That's about it, I guess," she finally finished softly. "When Harry disappeared with Miss Cole, it all hit the fan. I couldn't leave my parents' house without some reporter sticking a microphone in my face. Harry's office and all my files were locked down for the investigation, so I didn't really have a job anymore.

"Even though I had nothing to do with the embezzlement, who was going to trust me? I mean, I'd been
seeing another woman's husband, and the fact that her
father owns the company pretty well finished any
chance I might have had there."

Heat rose to her face, drying her eyes and parching
her throat. She couldn't look at either man, but Chad
remained steadfast beside her. He squeezed her hand
again, then dropped it to shift his chair closer and wrap
his arm around her shoulders.

She took a sip from the cola Duke had brought her
earlier and continued. "The telephone began ringing at
all hours. If it wasn't a reporter or a lawyer, it was
some nut accusing me of wrecking homes and under-
mining the moral structure of America, so I decided
to take off, too. They don't need me. I have no idea
how he took the company's funds, and with Miss Cole
in the picture, his wife won't have any trouble getting
her divorce."

Her shoulders rose and fell in a feeble shrug. "I
didn't want this ugliness spilling over onto my family
and thought if I left town it would all die down. I told
my folks I needed some time away and would be in
touch."

A thought occurred to her. "I haven't talked to them
since I hit Huntsville, though," she said slowly, then
cocked her head at Buck. "How did the police find
me?"

"You used your credit card in Wal-Mart last week."

"Oh."

Chad gave her shoulders a hug and asked, "Are you done for now, Buck?"

"Yeah." He punched the button to switch off the recorder. "You can take her home, but don't leave town, Miss Stallings."

Megan nodded and thought of the fresh-smelling sheets on the bed in her little room. She could curl up there and sleep for a week. She'd bolt the door and unplug the telephone—nothing and no one would get to her.

But on the return trip, Chad left the highway before they reached The Depot.

"Where are we going?"

"To the ranch. I thought you might want to let your folks know where you are."

"Thank you." Her voice was little more than a whisper.

"Megan?"

"What?"

He reached over to take her hand, enfolding it in his. "You weren't the one who broke up your boss's marriage."

"But . . ."

"Honey, he'd done that himself long before you appeared on the scene."

"How can you be so sure?"

"I'm not. Not really. But it seems to me that he'd need a little help hiding that kind of theft as long as he did. It's my guess the secretary helped him do it."

"You're probably right." Megan sat up straighter.

"Then they were most likely involved romantically the whole time."

"I'd say so, and God only knows how many there were before her. Harry destroyed his marriage all by himself."

"Poor Susan."

"Who?"

"His wife."

Chad grunted in agreement.

"Did I tell you she's pregnant?"

"The wife?"

"Yes. He swore they were estranged, but when I saw her at the office, it was easy to see he'd lied."

Chad pressed a kiss to her temple. "This whole scene must be pretty gruesome for you."

"To say the least."

"You going to be okay?"

"Yes." She sighed and leaned her head on his shoulder. "I'll get over the humiliation eventually. Just think how much worse it's got to be for Susan Thomas."

"You're quite a trooper, you know that, lady?"

"I'll bet you say that to all the women you pick up at the side of the road."

"Megan? Do you still love him?"

She lifted her head and studied his sharp profile. "No." With a finger, she traced the shape of his ear, then his strong jaw line. "I've come to realize that I really never did," she murmured.

He turned his head and met her gaze. "Oh?"

"Oh," she confirmed. "I know what love feels like now, and that wasn't it."

Chad steeled himself against the faint sounds of weeping coming from the front of the house. He'd settled Megan in the living room with a soft drink and the telephone, then retreated to the kitchen to give her some privacy. She'd been talking to her parents for nearly an hour now, the muffled crying having begun several minutes ago.

Maybe he should just look in on her. He started through the dining room and heard her say, "I'm sorry, Mama, I've made such a mess of things . . . I love you and Daddy too . . . Yes, I'll see you soon. Good-bye."

See them soon? She was leaving?

There's no reason for her to hide now, of course she'll be going home.

But *this* is her home!

No, it's your home. You only want to make *it hers.*

But I love her, confound it, and I know she loves me!

Maybe you'd better remind her of that.

He strode to the doorway, then paused. "Megan?"

She looked up and gave him a thin smile, quickly dashing away the remaining tears. "Thanks for the use of the phone, they were worried sick." She sniffled. "Seems it's in all the newspapers up there."

"I'm sorry, babe."

She stood and patted absently at her hair, obviously

a nervous gesture. "Yes, so am I. My parents are pretty upset about the whole thing."

"I can imagine."

She cast him a startled look.

"I mean, they had to have been frantic wondering what had happened to you. I know I was."

She walked to the front door and peered out the screen. Thunder rumbled from distant clouds. He came up behind her, but when he would have touched her shoulder, she pushed open the screen and stepped out onto the porch. He followed. Another roll of thunder. This one echoed around in his heart. She was leaving, he knew it, and it left him empty.

"I love to watch the rain moving in."

Her wistful tone seemed to him an affirmation that their time together would soon be over. He wrapped his arms around her waist from behind and pulled her back against his chest. Burying his face in her hair, he whispered desperately, "Don't go, Megan. I love you, you know I do."

She lay her head back against his shoulder and hugged his arms to her. "Chad, I have to."

"No you don't!"

She rubbed his jaw with her forehead, raising a hand to his other cheek. "Yes, I do. I was stupid and irresponsible, now I have to face the consequences."

"What about us?"

"There can be no us."

Megan felt him stiffen. Though she'd said it gently, he'd sucked in his breath as though she'd slapped him.

His arms dropped from around her and he stepped back. She immediately felt the loss.

Spinning, she grabbed his hand, stopping him from retreating into the house. "Chad, wait."

She struggled to explain. "I love you, too, but can't you see? This mess . . . I've got . . ."

Words failed her and she stumbled to a halt, her head lowered. She tried again, but all she could come up with was, "I'm sorry. You're such a wonderful man."

"Yeah, right," he spit out, his voice sharp with pain. "If I'm so blasted wonderful, why can't you stay with me?"

She traced his lips with her fingers as a cool breeze spun off the approaching storm and lifted a dark lock from his forehead. Her fingers trailed across his cheek and up into his hair, combing gently through it. She loved the feel of his hair, she thought irrelevantly, so thick and silky.

His eyes burned bright. Boiling ink, she thought again. Heavens, but she loved him so.

"Why?" he asked again.

Thunder sounded, closer, vibrating the air around them. "I'd just mess up your life," she whispered. "I don't want to do that to you, Chad."

"No, babe, no," he moaned. "Leaving me would mess it up, not staying."

She started to argue, but he snatched her to him. She wanted to soothe him, ease his hurt, reassure him.

She wanted to hide in his arms, out of sight of the
ugliness that pursued her.

Lightning split the air and thunder rattled the window panes as the sky opened up. Behind her, the rain
fell hard and heavy. Fat drops struck the dry ground
and bounced before settling again. In seconds the earth
was awash and torrents sluiced off the porch roof.

Megan pressed closer, wrapping her arms around
his neck. The storm overhead was no match for the
one battering her heart. Wind blew a spray off the
cascading rain, dampening their skin and clothing with
a fine mist.

They studied each other's eyes, lips, beloved features. Chad trailed gentle fingers down her cheek. His
hurt seemed to have lessened a little, but Megan could
still see the fear.

She wanted to tell him she'd stay, but she couldn't.
She'd been such a fool, and Chad deserved better than
that. Who knew, even Nadine could possibly make a
better go of a relationship than she, herself, had.

Almost as though he could read her mind, Chad's
brows curled and he growled, "No!" before clutching
her possessively to him again and burying his face in
her neck.

The wind picked up in earnest, washing rain across
the porch in waves. Chad scooped her up and into the
house before she realized his intent. He kicked the
front door shut behind them and was halfway up the
stairs before she could even register a thought.

This can't be happening. A man is not *carrying me*

up a staircase like in an old movie! But it was, he was.

He took her to a bedroom, his room she guessed, on the east side of the house and eased her down to sit on the bed. He crouched before her and when she started to speak, he stopped her words with his kiss. She tangled her fingers in his hair, and when she'd forgotten what she'd wanted to say, he raised his head.

"I love you," he whispered.

"But, Chad . . ."

He kissed her again, less pressured, less panicked, more persuasive.

"Chad . . ."

"I love you." And again a kiss. This one a little longer, a little sweeter. "I love you."

"Chad, you . . ."

It seemed the sure way to be kissed was to try to talk. She was on the verge of another monumental mess, and she knew it. But now she just didn't care.

This time when he raised his head, she vowed, "I love you."

A tender smile lifted his lips and he murmured, "Now you've got the idea."

He moved to stand up and she reached for him, but he slipped away and tugged her to her feet. "Come here," he urged, leading her to the window. He raised the shade and lifted the old wooden sash. The storm came from the north, so little moisture collected on the screen. He snagged a big old-fashioned rocking chair and dragged it up to face the window, then sat down and pulled her onto his lap.

"How's that?" he asked. "Now you have a ring-side seat." With a wave of his hand, he indicated the thunderstorm sweeping across the hills. Lightning, now more distant, danced in the clouds and the thunder rolled a timpani accompaniment.

She sighed and relaxed in his arms. "Will you come with me?"

He didn't need to ask where. "I'd like that." The wind whipped around the house, misting them with a spray of rain from time to time. Chad set the chair to rocking, but other than that, seemed perfectly content to simply hold her.

The harsh September sun reflected off the hood of her car, forcing Megan to squint against the glare. In spite of Chad's assurances to the contrary, she wondered again if summer weren't the only season available in this part of Texas. But hot sticky weather or not, she was happy. Deliriously so. Chad loved her.

They'd talked about a Thanksgiving wedding, which she would discuss with her parents. She and Chad were flying up to Kansas City in the morning. Right now, she had business to attend to.

Buck had declared her overqualified for waitressing and claimed he needed her business management skills to improve his portion of the operations. So for the past week she'd been learning about the fuel and mini-market side of The Depot. Reaching over, she straightened the file folder of tax forms on the seat beside her.

A believer in keeping a backup set of records, she'd printed up an extra set to be stored in the big old-fashioned safe at the ranch. She liked the challenge of her new job, and already Buck had implemented several of her marketing suggestions, such as moving some of the popular snacks to the back so the buyer was exposed to more of the inventory before making his selection, thus tempting him to pick up more.

A sharp whining noise drew her attention to the car, but before she had a chance to think what the latest trouble might be, the engine seized up and died. *Not again.* She coasted the little Ford to the shoulder of the road, muttering under her breath.

As she swung the door open, her senses were assaulted by the stench of automotive death. The air around her was heavy with the sticky smell of hot oil and scorched metal. The odor of overheated rubber stung her nostrils. She cast a glance skyward at the brilliant sun and sighed.

Oh, well, The Depot can't be more than a mile up the road. As she reached into the car for her purse, a passing pickup truck swerved to the shoulder several yards ahead of her, then backed quickly towards the front of her disabled car.

Doors slammed and a deep male voice chuckled. "Looks like the lady could use some help, boys."

Megan raised a hand to shield her eyes. A feeling

of unease prickled her skin as three men approached from the truck.

"My, my," another of the men offered, "if it ain't Miss High and Mighty. I wonder if Chad knows she's out here?"

"I doubt it," the first one answered. "We should probably look after her for him, don't you think?"

"Shoot," the third spoke up, "she's probably tired of him already. From what Nadine says he ain't much on keeping a woman interested, not even a prissy little thing like this."

"That right, darlin', has ole Chad let you down?"

The men advanced slowly as Megan took first one hesitant step back, then another. She'd recognized the unpleasant threesome from the diner as soon as she'd gotten a good look at their faces. Frantically, she scanned her surroundings. There was nowhere to run, no place to hide. Sporadic traffic flew by on the highway. Would anyone see? Would anyone notice she needed help?

She backed up another step and one of the men laughed. A low, nasty sound, it sent the chill of fear through her. *This can't be happening*, she thought as her heartbeats picked up rhythm. *I try to be so careful and now this? In broad daylight?*

"No!" She spun on her heel and began to run, but in only a few steps they had her. Rough hands snatched, grappling for a hold, bruising her skin as they hauled her to a stop. "No," she screamed again, in vain.

She bucked and twisted. A man on each arm, with the third close behind, they half-walked, half-dragged her back to their truck. She dug in her heels and pulled against the restraining hands with all of her strength. "Let me go!"

"Now is that any way to act?" The man at her back gave her a small shove. "Here we stop to help the lady and she gets all bent outta shape, what do you think of that, boys?"

The one with the nasty laugh chuckled again. "I think we ought to help her *unbend*, is what I think." His companions laughed in agreement.

"No! Stop it!" Anger and fear were quickly turning to stark terror. Megan growled in protest as they attempted to push her into the passenger side of the truck. The sun that had been so mercilessly hot only moments ago now seemed to wash her skin with ice. Blood pounded in her ears and her tongue adhered to the roof of her dry mouth.

I can't stop them! Dear God, they're really going to take me from the side of a public highway and I can't stop them! Help me, please, help me.

Chapter Ten

One man lifted Megan bodily but she thrashed and kicked so that he lost his grip. "Blasted spitfire," he muttered. The rest of his imprecation was drowned out by the sounds of an eighteen-wheeled truck downshifting rapidly, then locking up its brakes. The huge rig slid past in a grinding, hissing shower of gravel and dust, coming to rest at an angle from the roadway across the dirt shoulder. Its front portion barely missed the pickup truck, effectively pinning that vehicle in place between its great bulk and the smaller obstacle of Megan's car.

"Holy . . ." Megan's would-be abductor swallowed his curse. A massive figure advanced on them, boots striking the earth with heavy, ground-eating strides. A weighty tire iron was gripped in a ham-sized fist.

One of the cowboys rounded the hood of the smaller truck to head the giant off, but a wide set of knuckles lashed out and knocked him cold. The second cowboy lunged inside the truck and reappeared armed with a shotgun.

Megan, imprisoned in the third man's arms, yelled, "No!" She threw her weight back against her captor and kicked out with both feet as the armed cowboy raised the weapon. She'd managed to knock him off balance, but he recovered and raised the gun again, only to have it knocked from his grasp as his arm broke under the force of the descending tire iron.

His anguished scream split the air. As he lay writhing and moaning in pain, the wild-haired driver advanced on the one remaining cowboy, who held Megan in front of him like a shield.

"Mister," the giant rumbled, "I know for certain that lady don't belong to you, so I suggest you let go of her . . . *now*."

The cowboy looked frantically about then muttered, "Sure, sure," and shoved Megan into her rescuer's arms before turning to run. He hadn't figured on the big man's long reach though, and managed only one step before being pulled up short and off his feet by the back of his shirt. He landed hard on the packed dirt and was immediately pinned there by a heavy boot on his neck.

"I wouldn't move none, if I was you," the driver advised. Then he looked down at the woman whose hands were wrapped firmly around his right arm. "You okay, Meg?"

She shuddered and looked up into his face with a watery smile. "Thanks to you, I'm fine. I've never been so happy to see anyone in my entire life, Booth Harris."

Booth wrapped a brawny arm around her shoulders. "Does that mean you forgive me for tellin' Chad where to find you?" he teased.

"I owe you for that, too," she assured him.

"Booth Eugene Harris, why do you have that woman wrapped around you?"

The two jumped guiltily, then Booth grinned at the little dynamo glaring fiercely at him, one tiny fist planted on her hip. Her other arm cradled the discarded shotgun.

"Meg, I'd like you to meet . . ."

"Don't tell me." Megan laughed. "This just has to be your Billie."

"Yup."

"And you are?" the smaller woman asked too sweetly.

"Billie, darlin', calm down now," Booth soothed. "This here's Chad's gal, Meg. Remember, I told you about her?" He gave his diminutive wife a fond smile.

"Oh. Oh!" A genuine smile lit her pixie features and she quickly shifted the unwieldy gun to her left arm. "I'm so pleased to meet you," she declared as she grabbed Megan's hand and gave it an affectionate squeeze.

"Likewise," Megan replied.

The cowboy under Booth's foot began to make gagging sounds and the one he'd knocked cold was stirring. "Keep 'em covered, Billie," he instructed his wife as he pulled first one man, then the other to his feet and herded them to their truck.

"Get in there and sit quiet," he ordered and motioned the one with the broken arm to join his friends. He took the gun from Billie then and said, "Show Meg the baby and call for the county mounties, would ya darlin'."

"You've got Amy Jo with you?"

Billie grinned over her shoulder at Megan. " 'Course. It's easy when they're this age." She climbed up into the cab and took the baby from her safety seat and handed her down, then picked up the microphone to call Buck at The Depot.

The baby made a couple of mewling sounds and squirmed before settling in unfamiliar arms. Megan cuddled the infant close, gaining comfort from the warm little body. Giving her full attention to the precious bundle diverted Megan's thoughts from the horror she'd been trapped in mere moments ago.

"Breaker one nine for Little Bit."

Someone gave Booth's wife the air. "Go ahead Little Bit."

"Little Bit calling The Depot, are you there, Buck?"

Megan heard the familiar voice reply, "You got Buck here, what can I do for you, Little Bit?"

"A couple of things, actually. First off, we need the

county mounties about a mile south of your twenty. The Great Grizzly's got the drop on three sidewinders who tried to snatch a beaver off the gravel."

"What? Is the woman all right?"

"That's a roger. The second thing is, you might want to advise that Truck Stop Cowboy to loan his lady his ole pick 'em up truck so something like this don't happen again."

There were several seconds of dead silence, then Buck's shaken voice came back over the air waves. "You . . . you mean you're talkin' about Megan?"

"That's a roger, but she's fine, really. We'll bring her in with us if you want."

"Do that, and thanks. I'll have the mounties there pronto. Depot out."

In less than five minutes, three Walker County Sheriff's cars, four tow trucks and one Texas State Highway Patrol unit converged on the trio of vehicles at the side of the road. Billie was keeping the prisoners covered with the shotgun while Booth moved his rig so that it no longer blocked a lane of highway. He climbed down from the cab as the first sheriff's unit arrived. In less than six minutes, Chad arrived, skidding to a stop behind the last police car, bringing the number of vehicles clustered at the side of the highway to an even dozen.

The officer whose vehicle had been endangered glared at him from under the brim of his Stetson. "Winslow," he greeted dryly.

Chad nodded abruptly, not breaking his stride.

"I see you found her," the officer called out.

Chad turned and looked at him more closely, then gave Sims a sheepish grin. "Yeah, I did."

With all the emergency lights flashing, the area resembled a major disaster scene. Not that it almost wasn't, for Megan at least. She shuddered to think what might have happened if Booth hadn't come to her rescue. Even with the three lowlifes safely surrounded by peace officers, she stayed close to the large man's side while Billie murmured words of comfort beside her.

Shifting the baby to her shoulder, Billie pointed. "Look, here comes Chad."

Megan knew he was there, she'd spotted his truck a half mile away, and her attention had riveted on him the moment he stepped from the cab. She watched his long strides devour the distance between them, waiting for him to reach her, unable to move from Booth's protective shadow until he did. She knew it was reaction setting in, and that she'd be all right, but for now she stood rooted in place, needing Chad's arms more than anything in this world.

He stopped not two feet from her. "Babe?"

She flung herself against him and burst into tears as his arms closed around her. "Are you all right? Are you hurt?" He ran his hands over her arms, her back, her head, her face, seeking the answers to questions she couldn't respond to through her sobs.

"She's fine," Billie assured him, "just scared. Booth

got to her before that scum even had a chance to get her in their truck."

Chad clasped the big man's shoulder with one hand. "I owe you, I owe you big time. Thanks," he muttered, his voice gruff with emotion.

Booth pulled Billie to his side and smiled. "Don't mention it. You'd do the same for me."

"In a heartbeat," Chad agreed. He hugged Megan tightly, then ducked his head to look in her face. "Hey," he teased gently, "are you about to wind down? You're making a lot of men nervous here with all that bawling."

Megan sniffled indelicately and scowled at him from beneath wet lashes.

"Well, you know how it is," he continued teasing, "men just don't know what to do with a weeping female. It scares the heck out of us."

"Yeah, right." She dried her eyes with the handkerchief he offered and blew her nose.

"Better now?" He rested his hand on the back of her neck.

"Yes, I'm fine."

"Stay with Booth while I see what we have to do before we can go home," he instructed and dropped a kiss on her nose before striding back down the caravan.

His steadying touch had been all she needed. She watched him stop and talk to the Sergeant, then move to the knot of wrecker drivers. Soon he was back, his strong arm securing her to his side. "You'll need to give a statement. The charge will be attempted kidnapping." He looked apologetically at Booth. "They'll need a statement from you, too. Sorry."

Booth smiled. "No problem. I'll just give 'em a call at the other end to say we'll be a little late. This load'll be just as good then as it is now."

Chad shook the big man's hand. "Thanks. For everything." He squeezed Megan's waist then and instructed, "Give me your keys, I'm having your car towed."

She dug the keys from her purse then exclaimed, "Oh, get the tax files out of the front seat. If I lose those your father will kill me."

"Not likely, sweetheart. Anything else you need out of there before we get back next week?"

"Not that I can think of."

He retrieved the folder, then tossed the keys to the man waiting to haul the little car away. Another of the tow trucks prepared to hook up the would-be abductors' vehicle as the prisoners were being marched to the waiting cruisers.

Traffic on the highway crawled by as the curious slowed to see what was going on. Chad shook his head. "For one small woman, you sure can cause a spectacle, you know that?"

Megan's startled eyes met his. "You're not blaming me for what happened?"

He laughed, just from the joy of knowing she was safe. "No, babe, not by a long shot."

They walked, hand in hand, along the line of trucks

and cars. "It's a good thing Booth came riding to the rescue. I'll bet he was surprised to see it was me."

"I doubt it."

"Why do you say that?"

"He recognized your car."

"That's ridiculous."

"Nope."

She pulled up next to the last police car, the one in front of Chad's truck. "Why on earth would Booth Harris have any idea what my car looks like?"

Chad stuffed his hands in the back pockets of his jeans and scuffed at a rock with the toe of his boot. "Because, I had everyone within earshot of my CB radio looking for your car when you took off."

"You what?"

"Not only that," interrupted a young deputy, "he darn near got himself run in for cruising the college campus. We thought we had a pervert on our hands."

Megan turned her startled gaze back to Chad. "He's kidding, right?"

" 'Fraid not. Megan, meet Officer Sims. He's the one who stopped me."

"Stopped you? For driving through the campus?"

Chad shrugged. "I was looking for you. I'd already been to all the hotel and motel parking lots several times and decided to add the school to my list."

"Oh Chad, *all* the hotels and motels? Surely not."

"Every last one of them, I swear. Several more than once."

"I had no idea you'd gone to so much trouble."

He gave a mirthless bark of laughter and continued, "Then there were the hours spent on the telephone checking with all the apartment complexes, and the driving around chasing down leads."

"Chad, no!"

He shrugged his shoulders expressively and his voice dropped to a husky rasp. "I couldn't face losing you, babe. I had to find you."

She wrapped her arms around his waist and hugged, pressing her cheek against the wall of his chest. "No wonder you looked like death warmed over that night. I'm sorry I've caused you so much trouble."

"Yeah, well that's over now, right?"

"Right," she agreed, then remembered her manners. "It's nice to meet you, officer."

Sims tipped his hat. "The pleasure is mine, ma'am, and call me Ted." He swung his gaze back to Chad. "Can't say as I blame you a bit, Winslow. But if all this is any indicator, you might as well be on a first-name basis, too. I do believe the little lady is going to keep you busy."

Chad broke out laughing and slapped Sims on the shoulder. "Lord, I hope not," he groaned. "Not like this anyway."

Megan humphed and marched to Chad's pickup. He stopped laughing when he heard her slam the door.

Sims winked at him. "Better get her out of here before something else happens."

* * *

Stars glittered in a sky devoid of moonlight. A cool breeze washed the last of the day's lingering heat from the air, stirring the leaves of the oak trees that sheltered the house. Sitting on the second porch step, Megan leaned back into the protective cradle of Chad's body and sighed, settling between his knees. He sat on the level above her, his arms wrapped lightly around her shoulders. Dropping a kiss on the crown of her head, he broke their silence to ask, "Nervous about going home?"

"A little."

"They aren't going to hurt you, you know."

"The lawyers, the reporters, or my family?" she asked dryly.

He chuckled and gave her a reassuring hug. "Any of them. The authorities just need your statements, you don't even have to talk to the reporters, and your family loves you."

She sighed again and rested her head back against his chest. "You're right, I suppose."

"Hey," he changed the subject, "if you could have your car painted any color you wanted, what would you like?"

"You're kidding."

"No, I just thought Jim could give me an estimate on that too, when he worked up the one for the engine repair."

"That car isn't worth fixing and you know it. Besides, I'm almost as broke as when I first got here."

"Oh, for Pete's sake, we're going to be married in a couple of months, I'll take care of your car."

"That's awfully sweet of you, but I can't let . . ."

"I said I'll take care of it," he repeated, his tone allowing no argument. "I might even have him throw a coat of paint on Grandpop's pickup."

"Okay." She tilted her face up and kissed his jaw. "Thank you."

Chad caught her chin and lowered his mouth over hers for a quick kiss. He raised his head and smiled. "Now, what color do you want?"

"Blue?" she asked, her voice thready. "I like that pretty, bright sky-blue."

"Sound good, I'll see what we can do."

Her fingertips traced his jaw, then brushed over his lips. "I love you, Chad Winslow."

"I know," he whispered, "I love you, too."

Megan glanced around to make certain they weren't leaving anything behind. Chad and Buck were loading the luggage for the drive to the Houston airport. In a few short hours she'd be introducing Chad to her family . . . and in only two months she'd be Mrs. Chad Winslow! She could still hardly believe it.

The telephone rang and she answered. "Mrs. Winslow?" a voice asked.

Distracted, she replied, "Yes."

"This is Emma in Doctor Blake's office. Congratulations. Your tests are back and everything looks fine. Doctor said to tell you you're looking at an early April delivery date and he wants to see you again in two months, okay?"

Megan was too stunned to answer.

"Do you want to make an appointment now?"

"Ah . . ." Shock reduced her voice to a mere croak and her mind to vacant space. A giant fist gripped her chest, squeezing the air from her body. She groped blindly for a handhold as buckling knees dropped her to the arm of the sofa.

"Mrs. Winslow? Nadine?"

No! No, she wasn't. "Ah, no. Not right now, thank you," she murmured, then hung up. *Nadine's pregnant.*

Nadine is pregnant!

Megan's key protective instinct kicked in. Flight. Escape the danger. Hide from the pain. She had to get home.

You are going home. Today. Just get on that plane as though nothing's happened. In a few hours you'll be with your family again and you'll be fine.

She clutched her purse tightly against her body to still her shaking hands and stepped out onto the porch.

"Got everything?" Buck asked.

She nodded. Chad stood by his father's Suburban, holding the front passenger door open for her. She walked past him and reached for the back seat door handle.

"You don't want to sit in front?" he asked.

"No, I'm going to try to catch a nap."

Chad reached to help her into the large vehicle and

felt her stiffen under his touch. His eyes sought hers, but she averted her face.

"Uh, Chad?"

"Yeah?" He spoke to the back of her head.

"You don't really need to make this trip, you know. There's so much you have to do around here, I'll be fine on my own."

What the heck? "I want to go, you know that," he assured her, then added, "besides, we've got a wedding to plan."

Was she really that nervous about seeing her parents again, he wondered? Probably just the combined stress of everything she'd been through lately. Not that he blamed her for being uptight. She'd shown a great deal of courage yesterday in the face of an attempted abduction. From what Booth had told him, she'd been a first-rate, kicking, screaming wildcat. He closed her door and climbed into the front seat, smiling to himself as he imagined the scene Booth had described. His Megan was quite a woman all right.

Soon they'd be headed for the airport so she could return to her former hometown and face down more unpleasantness. Heck, it'd be strange if she *weren't* a little anxious, given all she'd been through. He turned to look at her as his father opened the other door and slid behind the steering wheel.

She'd leaned her head back on the seat and her eyes were closed. "You okay, babe?" She nodded, but didn't answer.

Buck raised his eyebrows in query.

"She's going to rest a bit," Chad explained.

The older man grunted in approval.

At the airport, they checked the luggage and headed down the long concourse for their departure gate. Chad reached for Megan's hand as they walked, but she danced away from his touch like a skittish foal. He frowned and his hand fell, empty, to his side. She hadn't spoken a word since leaving the ranch.

The gate attendant checked them in and Chad followed Megan to a bank of chairs facing the big windows. She hesitated and he sat. Instead of joining him though, she advanced to the expanse of plate glass overlooking the runway and took up a post between two groups of excited children.

Her distancing hurt. *Give her some room. Face it, you don't really know her all that well. This is probably her normal reaction to trouble. Some women you've known throw tantrums, Megan clams up. She needs you to be here for her, though, so do just that. Sit quietly in the background until she needs you.*

Their plane taxied up to the gate and discharged its arriving passengers. The attendant announced the boarding of special needs travelers and those with children. Megan continued to watch out the window. The first section of regular passengers was called and still she didn't move. When their section was announced, she turned slowly from the wall of glass and moved to the doorway without bothering to join him in the line.

Chad worked his way down the aircraft aisle to where she was already seated, gazing out a window. Silently he slipped into the seat beside her, and wondered what he could do or say to break the downward spiral in her mood. Should he just leave her alone to work through whatever was bothering her, or should he try to get her to talk? Maybe he'd just wait and see what happened, he didn't know what he could say anyway. Once they were airborne she'd probably relax. His arm brushed hers as he fastened his seat belt and she shifted away. He frowned but again said nothing.

Chapter Eleven

Megan was suffocating. Would this flight never end? Tears clogged her throat and the effort it took to hold them back had her jaw and neck muscles knotted like rope. Her temples throbbed with excruciating intensity. Sitting next to Chad in such a confined space was almost more than she could bear. The colossal jerk. One more in an illustrious line.

Well, it'd be a short line. She'd give up before going through this again. Obviously her mechanism for choosing a mate was seriously flawed. Two men, two losers. Next time she'd let someone else do the picking. If there ever was a next time. If she had an ounce of sense left, there wouldn't be.

She pressed her forehead against the cool glass of the small window. Clouds looked so different from this side. Instead of the rolling, dumpling-shaped bottoms they presented to the earth, the tops exactly resembled banks of snow. Piles of white heaped high and stained a dingy gray along the edges; dirty snow, scraped from the streets and mounded up by snowplows.

It would be several more weeks before they had snow at home. She doubted Huntsville, Texas, ever saw it at all.

Something touched her hand and she jumped. Chad. She'd managed to think of something else for a moment, why couldn't he have left her alone?

"Babe?"

Megan didn't turn from the window. "Hum?"

"What's wrong?"

She just shook her head.

"It might help if you talk."

How could he? How on earth could he sit there and ask so sweetly about her problems? She thought she'd scream. Literally. At the realization, panic chilled her body and roiled her stomach. An acid taste burned her throat. It *was* entirely possible that she would break out screaming in the middle of this flight! A shudder ran through her frame.

Chad's arm came around her shoulders, pulling her against him. "Calm down," he murmured in her ear, "it's going to be all right."

It's going to be all right. If only it were. Once before she'd trusted him to explain, to clear up the misunderstanding, to fix things so they could be together.

But he'd lied and this was something that couldn't be fixed.

You didn't "fix" a baby. Nadine was pregnant and Megan would not be the one to deprive that child of its father, no matter how badly she wanted Chad.

She allowed the embrace, even turned her head to hide against his shoulder. She couldn't lose control, she had to get a grip. Another shudder racked her and Chad tightened his hold. Snug in his arms, she drew a deep breath, one rich with his scent. Tears pooled on the edge of her lids.

It made no sense. More than anything in the world, she wanted to be right where she was, safe in Chad's arms. But what kind of reasoning called this safe? It was from Chad himself that she needed sanctuary. He'd lied to her! She loved him and he'd lied to her. Oh, she couldn't rightly claim he'd betrayed her, because Nadine *was* his wife, after all. But he hadn't been truthful about his relationship with that wife.

She smoothed a trembling hand up his chest and latched onto the lapel of his linen sport coat. Like a child with a security blanket, she focused on the coat's texture, rubbing her thumb repeatedly over the lightly slubbed surface in an attempt to block out all other thought. Tears traced her cheeks, but she bit down hard on the sobs.

Why? Why? Why? The one word question ran like a litany through her mind. Why had he lied? Nadine had been pregnant before Megan had ever heard of Huntsville, before she and Chad had ever laid eyes on one another. He could have said it was over. *Like Harry.*

After all, she knew there'd been women in his life before she came along. He didn't need to lie and say he'd never touched his wife. *Like Harry.* Another shudder snaked its way down her spine and Chad responded by folding her as closely into his body as he could. His cheek pressed down on her bowed head and he whispered soothing sounds.

Oh, God, how am I going to live without him? I asked You not to let me make a mistake this time, didn't You hear me?

The thought occurred to Megan that maybe she'd been the one not listening. Had the answer been one she didn't want to hear, so she'd tuned it out? It seemed a strong possibility.

"Honey?" Chad's breath feathered her ear. "We're almost there, you need to get hold of yourself."

A large hand cupped the side of her head, pressing it to his chest. "Did you hear me, babe?"

She nodded and Chad's arms slowly withdrew and he tilted forward to retrieve a handkerchief from his hip pocket. She realized then that he knew she'd been crying.

The plane landed and Megan preceded Chad down the passenger way. Objects seemed too bright, as though spotlighted, voices too loud, a crescendo of noise with no pattern or meaning. Is this what it's like to have a nervous breakdown, she wondered? Though outwardly composed, she was holding to her self-control by a mere thread.

Her steps faltered and Chad's hand came up to steady her. How ironic, to be supported by the very man who'd knocked her whole world out of kilter! She fought the hysterical need to giggle. No doubt at all, she was losing it.

"Meggie!" Her father swooped down on her, beefy arms opened wide, his eyes alight with pleasure.

She'd made it! She was home. With an anguished cry, she threw herself against the man who'd made everything right in her universe since before she could remember. He swung her around and she burst into tears, giving in to the gut-wrenching sobs she'd suppressed since hanging up the telephone back in Huntsville.

"Meggie? Meggie, what's wrong? What is it baby?"

Her arms locked tightly around her father's neck, Megan's feet dangled a couple of inches off the ground. She knew she should let go, should dry her eyes and behave like the adult she was, but her body wouldn't respond. Her arms clung tighter and the sobs became more tortured.

She heard her mother's practical voice coax softly, "Let's take her over here, Charles." Her father moved, with her still clinging like an ivy to his husky body, her face buried in the side of his neck. He settled her in a chair and ducked out of her stranglehold. She opened her eyes to find him squatting in front of her, bandanna in hand, face tight with concern. Chad stood in the background looking on.

"Take it easy, baby," her father soothed, pressing the blue handkerchief on her, "everything's gonna be okay, you'll see."

"Of course it is," her mother agreed. She took the seat beside Megan and patted her hand. "She's just letting off a little of the tension. She'll be fine in a minute."

Megan tried to give her worried father a reassuring smile, but failed miserably. *She wouldn't be fine. Not in a minute, not in a hundred years.* She glanced up at Chad, waiting stoically in the background. How did he do it? How did he manage to look so solid, so handsome, so . . . wonderful when he'd destroyed her world and reduced her to a sodden mess?

More importantly, how had *she* let it happen? Making use of her father's oversized handkerchief, Megan tidied herself, then drew in a long shaky breath. She lifted her chin and struggled for a firm controlled tone.

"Mother, Daddy, this is Chad Winslow."

Chad stepped forward, hand extended, as her father stretched to his feet. The men shook hands.

"When are we going to tell them?"

Megan swung around, startled. She'd managed to avoid being alone with Chad since their arrival, and right now he was supposed to be at the hardware store with her father. She'd taken this opportunity to spend a few quiet minutes in the family room. Watching the birds gathered around the feeder off the patio had always been one of her favorite ways to unwind.

He studied her a moment, a small frown easing its way across his features, darkening the eyes she'd loved so well. He must have detected something in her expression. The frown deepened. "You've changed your mind?"

Resting his hand on the back of her father's recliner as though needing to steady himself, he correctly read the answer in her silence. "I wondered why you were avoiding me, but I thought it was still just nerves . . . it never occurred to me . . ." He broke off in evident confusion, the light in his eyes dulling.

Megan wanted to die. She crossed her arms and hung on tight, willing it to all be over. She'd been through so many scenes lately, but this would be the worst.

"Why, Megan?" he demanded, his voice a raw whisper. "Why?"

"Yes, why?" she snapped in return. "Why did you lie to me? Did you think I wouldn't find out?"

In a voice as pained as his, she pressed on. "Maybe it was only once, and since it happened before we'd even met it didn't count? You can't exactly get an annulment now, can you? Or were the two of you going to lie on official documents?"

He took a step towards her, his hand outstretched. "What are you talking about? What lie?"

"The lie about your hands-off marriage! I know Nadine is having a baby, Chad!"

"A baby? She can't be! I always . . ."

Megan cut him off. "The doctor's office called just before we left. They thought I was her. Congratulations," she sneered, grief making her voice cruel, "you'll be a daddy the first of April."

Chad's hands clenched at his sides. His face rigid with suppressed emotion, he spoke with precise tones. "There's got to be some mistake, a mix-up of some sort."

"Oh, there was a mistake all right, and I made it. I'm sorry you came all this way for nothing, but I tried to get you to let me make the trip alone," she reminded him, her expression cold, her tone brittle. "I think it would be a good idea if you went back to Texas as soon as possible."

He glared at her. A muscle worked in his jaw. "We aren't finished, Megan."

"I am. I have nothing more to say."

"I don't mean this conversation, I mean us, you and me. We aren't finished."

Megan tipped up her chin and fought to hide her broken heart behind a scathingly haughty tone. "*There* you are mistaken, Chad Winslow. We are quite finished. Once again, the specter of your wife has intervened."

She pushed past him and fled up the stairs to lock herself in her bedroom.

Chad watched her go, fury flushing his body with heat while some other emotion raked his heart with razor-like talons.

Pregnant! Where in the hot fires of Hades had she come up with that one? It was just an excuse. It had to be. An excuse to shut him out, to send him on his way. He'd done it again. He'd played the patsy for some conniving woman. He'd been taken in by her sweet smile, her little-girl-lost look, her gentle manner. Her touch, her kisses.

With an oath he slammed both fists down on the cushioned back of the chair, then stalked from the room. Taking the stairs two at a time, he followed in her wake, heard her bedroom door slam in the upper hall. He wanted to kick down that door and make her admit she was lying. He wanted to hold her until all the hurt went away. His and hers.

Instead, he turned in the other direction to the guest room. When he'd packed and called for a taxi, he called The Depot to arrange for someone to meet him at the Houston airport. To his profound relief, Jamie answered. The questions would wait until he got home.

"Something to drink, sir?"

Chad jumped at the stewardess' interruption of his black musings. "Yeah," he growled, "a bourbon. Double."

The woman gave him a wary glance and poured the drink. Good, he thought grimly, at least one woman on this earth didn't see him as a prize dupe created just for her tiny feet to walk all over. He took a generous swallow and grimaced as the alcohol burned its way down his throat. He didn't usually drink hard liquor, and certainly not this early in the afternoon.

He nursed the remainder of the drink. It wouldn't do to arrive in Houston drunk, he'd have enough questions to answer without that, and he had no idea what to tell anyone. His folks would respect his privacy, but after all they'd done for Megan he owed them some kind of explanation. The truth, he supposed. It was all he had.

The woman had taken the sanctuary they'd offered, taken the loving support she'd needed during a difficult time, and now that he'd delivered her safely back to the bosom of her family, had no further need of any of them.

Not that he or his folks ever attached strings to helping someone, but confound it! Did she have to take his heart in the bargain? Did she really need to reclaim her self-esteem by racking up one more conquest?

What now, what now? He laid his head back and closed his eyes. The future stretched endlessly before him, a murky void. He envisioned an empty road, snaking gently off into the cloudy distance; no trees, no colors, no light. Everything empty, completely barren. *Ah, Megan, what have you done?*

It took a woman like her, warm, sweet, fresh as spring, to destroy a man. Her kind just sort of snuck in and set up house in a man's heart without him knowing until way too late. Nadine's kind were safer, they were obvious. A man knew up front that if he played, he paid. *But Megan . . . oh, God, Megan . . .*

It had been awhile since Chad had last prayed, and he remembered Megan had been the reason then, too.

A car horn sounded at the curb and moments later she heard the front door shut. Megan's heart thundered in her ears and the pressure built in her chest. Chad was leaving, she had only this final chance to catch a glimpse of him. To admire one last time that confident, long-legged stride, the tilt of his head, the squaring of his shoulders. To see the wind ruffling his rich dark hair.

Instead, she clutched her pillow tightly in both fists and fought the urge to rush to her bedroom window. The taxi pulled away and she released the breath she'd been holding, only to draw it back in a great gulping sob. How much heartache could a body stand? How much disillusionment before one's psyche was irreparably damaged? Surely she'd reached her limit? She buried her face in the pillow and cried herself to sleep.

"Son, are you sure you're not making a mistake? That doesn't really sound like Meg."

Chad looked across the kitchen table at his mother. "Well how would *you* see it? Just as soon as she'd squared things with her folks, she shut me down. One minute we're talking wedding plans and the next she's throwing me out on my ear."

"Wedding plans?"

"Yeah." He studied the pale bubbles rising to the neck of his beer bottle. Little pockets of air seeking an escape from their liquid imprisonment. Strange to identify with something so common and inanimate.

"Chad?" his mother prompted.

He sighed and tipped the bottle to his lips, then wiped away the lingering moisture with his thumb. "We were going to check with her folks on the possibility of a Thanksgiving wedding." He could tell by the look in her eyes that his flat tone and bland expression didn't fool his mother for a minute.

"I see. Then I'd better start looking for a dress."

"Mom . . ."

She interrupted his protest to pat his hand. "It's going to work out. You love her and that's what counts, not the misunderstandings or the stubborn pride."

He exploded to his feet, sending his chair sliding into the wall. "What stubborn pride? She doesn't want me, she was just using us as a place to hide out! I can't marry the woman if she won't have me."

"But you could marry a woman *you* didn't want?"

A scowl knit his brows and he turned to the pace the kitchen. "It's not the same and you know it," he muttered, then swung back to face his mother. "And that's another thing! Megan made up some story about Nadine being pregnant. She couldn't even admit the truth! She had to have a lie to justify kicking me out. As if I'd ever touch that conniving . . ." In deference to his parent, he left the sentence unfinished.

"Nadine's pregnant?"

"I don't know. It's the first I'd heard of it."

"What made Meg think so?"

He ran his fingers through his hair as he tried to remember what she'd said. "A phone call, I think. Yeah, that was it. She said the doctor's office called here and thought she was Nadine. Then she 'congratulated' me and said I'd be a father in April."

"But you're not . . . ?"

"Of course not! I've always told her I wasn't interested." He crossed the kitchen with agitated strides, then turned and retraced his path.

"Well someone was."

Chad came to an abrupt halt.

He slumped down in the chair and began to toy with the bottle in front of him. "Nadine's a real piece of work, isn't she?"

"You could say that. I don't understand how you can even begin to lump Meg in the same category."

"I didn't," he protested.

His mother simply raised an eyebrow.

"I don't understand what's going on. What am I supposed to do?"

"First, you have to quit going off like firecrackers on a hot stove. You can't figure anything out when you're exploding in a dozen different directions. It's obviously a misunderstanding, and given Meg's past history, I'd say she's running scared. As scared as you are."

He concentrated his attention on peeling the label off the bottle, scraping it with his thumbnail. His mother's touch on his hand brought his gaze back to hers.

"It's no sin to be scared, son. You love her and don't want to lose her. But sitting here stewing isn't the answer. In the end you may be right, she may not want you, but will that be any worse than what you're going through now? If you want that girl, you're going to have to solve the puzzle and take her the answer, Chad. If you want her, you're going to have to fight for her."

His gaze focused on the colorful foil he nudged from the sweating bottle, but his mind was on Megan. He barely heard the footsteps crossing the kitchen and the back door clicking shut behind his mother. She'd called it a puzzle, one he had to solve, but lordy he was weary. So eternally weary. He hadn't felt this tired, this drained, since the day Megan had run away.

Megan. Would she always put him through a wringer like this? He lifted the bottle to his lips and drank deeply, then smiled. *She will . . . if I can get her back.*

"Megan got your phone call by mistake and she thinks I'm the father."

Nadine's mouth curled in a cat-like smile and she spread one hand to study her lacquered nails. "Well now, that's a natural assumption, isn't it," she fairly purred. "After all, you *are* my husband."

Air hissed between his clenched teeth in a sharply drawn breath. "Not in this life, or any other! Your little stunt with Dex's scanner and computer had me going there for a few days, but I've never laid so much as a finger on you, and we both know it."

Nadine tossed her head and propped one hand on her hip. He didn't like the glint in her wicked eyes. "Prove it," she challenged softly.

"What?"

She shrugged one shoulder with a provocative motion. "Prove it's not yours, husband dearest."

"That's not too hard these days," he reminded her.

"What, DNA testing? You're right, no problem, but you've got a few months to wait." A long thin cigarette trailed smoke from between ring-festooned fingers. She lifted it to her lips and took a lazy drag, then tipped her head back to release the cloud into the air. "Is sweet little Meg going to hang around, twiddling her thumbs waiting for you?"

"Why, Nadine? What's the point?" He leaned one hand against the rough cinderblock wall at the back of the building and scowled down at the little conniver. A dry breeze ruffled his hair.

"It's not like there was ever anything between us. Besides the fact that I could have you charged with forgery if you don't back off, aren't you looking forward to your move to Austin?"

The one shoulder rose again in a shrug. She dropped her cigarette in the dirt and ground it to crumbs with a twist of her foot. "I'm not going."

Chad gritted his teeth. "What do you mean you're not going?"

"There's been a change of plans," she cooed, patting her flat stomach.

"But what about—"

"Oh, come on," she snapped, obviously tiring of her cat and mouse game. "It's gonna take more than a lousy three thousand to get rid of me now. If you want me gone, you'll pay for it, stud! Big time."

"Why you—"

"Ah ah ah, no name calling." She waggled one obscenely long claw back and forth. "After all, I *am* the mother of your child."

"Not even when Hell freezes over!"

Her trill of laughter raced up his spine, then slowly slid back down like the icy finger of death, chilling him bone deep in spite of the warm fall sunlight. His hands bunched into fists at his sides and the vision of strangling the woman before him took on the proportions of a long-denied quest.

It was blackmail, ugly and simple, but for Megan he'd pay it. "How much?" he snarled. "How much will it take for me to never see your face again?"

Chapter Twelve

Nadine had to be crazy, he didn't have that kind of money. *Ten thousand,* she'd said. *You get me ten thousand dollars and I'm out of your life forever.* Not that he couldn't raise it, but it would take time. Time he didn't have. He knew that with each passing day the gulf between Megan and himself grew wider.

He could include a few of the cows in his fall sale of steers. He hated to do that, they were the future of the herd. But without Megan he had no future.

Horses! He could part with a couple of them . . . Maybelle and Rowdy. No, not Maybelle. She was Megan's.

Chad snapped the pencil between his fingers and threw the pieces at the calculator. They bounced off the kitchen table and rolled across the floor.

Who was he kidding? The only way to get that much money as quickly as he needed it, was to take out a loan. He'd have to mortgage his portion of the ranch. The land his grandfather had left to him.

Megan stood at the glass door and watched as a wet autumn wind prodded skeletal tree branches into a macabre dance. Like bony fingers, the naked limbs gestured against a background of gray clouded sky. At the edge of the patio, her father's bird feeder leaned in dismal neglect; empty, forgotten. Like her, she thought. Just like her.

She crossed her arms and drew a shaky breath. Forgotten, but not forgetting. Not yet at any rate. She'd known it would take some time to get over Chad, but never imagined it would be this bad. Even now a tear slipped free and she dashed it away in annoyance. Blast it! Would she never stop crying?

She turned from the dreary view. What now? What on earth was she to do with her life now? Of course her parents were happy to have her back, insisted she could stay as long as she liked, but that was no answer. She had to get a job, a place of her own.

A life.

And she would, she really would. But not today. Today she was just too tired to deal with it. A fire beckoned cheerily from the family room hearth. The mantle was decorated with dried corn and colorful gourds. A cornucopia-shaped basket spilled forth apples and nuts. Thanksgiving was only four days away.

Thanksgiving! We wanted to be married at Thanksgiving, but he hasn't even called. Not once. She choked back a sob and pressed a fist to her lips. *Is he painting a nursery, hanging teddy bear borders? Stop it! Just stop it!* But she couldn't quit torturing herself. Her imagination, always fertile, presented her with a picture of Nadine, body swollen with child, snug in Chad's embrace as they surveyed a fresh, bright nursery.

Oh, dear God! She couldn't take this anymore. She'd never been a weepy female, but it seemed to be all she did lately!

She stumbled up the stairs and flung herself onto her bed, where she buried her face in her pillows, glad she was the only one home. For long minutes she gave herself up to the anger, the frustration . . . the grief, of having loved Chad Winslow. The tears flowed and her lungs labored for air as she sobbed and wailed, occasionally screaming into the bedding she pummeled with her fists.

No more holding back. She'd get that cowboy out of her system if it was the last thing she ever did! Even if it meant crying herself into a state of hoarse dehydration.

Eventually, her emotional stores depleted, she rolled to her back and threw an arm across her aching eyes, blocking the subdued afternoon light. From the upstairs hall, the telephone rang. She ignored it.

After the fifth ring, she realized her mother hadn't turned on the answering machine before leaving. *Of course not, she knew I'd be home.* Two more rings and the instrument fell silent. Megan gently pressed her fingertips against her swollen eyes, then rose to get a cold washcloth to soothe them.

While in the bathroom, she took a couple of aspirin, then carried the wet cloth back to her bedroom. She fluffed her pillows and lay down. The cool cloth eased the ache and she exhaled an exhausted sigh. *Okay, that's over with, now back to the important question. What now?* Counting her options like sheep, she dozed off.

Oh, for Pete's sake! Megan levered herself up on her elbows. The telephone was ringing again, its summons imperative through her open door. She threw her legs over the side of the bed and winced when her head throbbed in protest. The phone had time for another ring and a half before she grabbed up the receiver.

"Hel . . ." Her voice rasped from her abused vocal chords and she had to clear her throat before she tried again. "Hello?"

"Hello, may I speak with Meg Stallings, please?" The woman's voice was gentle, with a touch of drawl to it.

"This is she."

"Meg? It didn't sound like you, dear. This is Eileen Winslow, how have you been?"

"Eileen! Oh, ah, fine, how about you?"

Eileen chuckled. "Me? Confused mostly. I expected

you to come back after you got business up there taken care of. We miss you."

Megan swallowed against a sudden lump in her throat. "That . . . that's really sweet, but I've, uh, decided to stay here. My parents, you know . . ."

"I understand, dear. You do what you have to do, just know you have a place here anytime you want it."

"Thank you. How . . . how is . . . everyone?"

"Well, let's see. Buck and I are fine, Alma's arthritis is acting up, Jamie got the scholarship to Sam Houston he applied for . . ."

Megan gritted her teeth. *Chad! How is Chad? Does he miss me too? Does he even remember me?*

". . . Celia's youngest is getting married the first of the year. Guess that about does it, except for the fact that Chad's got me worried."

Megan's heart lodged somewhere in her airway. "Chad? What's wrong with Chad?"

"I wouldn't say anything is wrong, exactly. It's just that he's taken the fool notion to mortgage his part of the ranch. With the economy the way it is, I'm afraid he's running the risk of losing a lot of money, maybe even his land."

"Mortgage his land? But why?"

"Oh, something to do with Nadine. He says she's expecting and needs ten thousand dollars." Eileen paused and gave a disgusted huff. "I know maternity costs are up these days, but it sounds more like blackmail to me."

Squeezing her eyes tightly shut, Megan struggled to

sound strong, normal. "So you're going to be a grand-mother? Congratulations."

"Nonsense," Eileen snapped. "That baby's not Chad's and you know it as well as I do."

"I *don't* know it! If the baby's not Chad's why is he paying for it?" Megan argued. She added softly, "And why hasn't he called?" before realizing one thing had nothing to do with the other. Just because he wasn't the father of Nadine's child didn't mean he wanted anymore to do with herself. Not after the way she'd thrown him out.

"What he's paying for, is a tendency to help the world," Eileen muttered in disgust. "Like I said, I be-lieve this is blackmail. Literally."

"But what would Nadine have to hold over him?"

Eileen snorted. "You, of course."

"Me? I don't understand." Megan rubbed her fore-head, her fingertips lightly skimming back and forth over her puckered brow. On the other end of the line, Eileen exhaled with a heavy sigh.

"It's simple, girl. Nadine knows once the baby's born, it'll be a snap to prove Chad's not the father, but it'll be too late for him. She figures you'll be out of the picture by then." The older woman paused, then asked, "She's right, isn't she? You haven't called him either, have you?"

"No, I haven't," Megan admitted. "I . . . I thought he'd lied to me."

"Thought so."

"But, Eileen, that still doesn't explain his need to mortgage the land."

"Way I've got it figured, if Chad pays her the money, Nadine's supposed to come clean with you about her baby's paternity."

"That's it? All that money just for her confession?"

"My boy loves you, Meg," Eileen replied, her voice tender. "Don't doubt that for a minute. He'll do what he feels is needed to get you back."

Silence, heavy and solid, stretched the distance, humming along the lines.

"Meg?"

"I . . . I love him, too," came the soft, breathy reply.

"So. What're you goin' to do?"

Megan sighed. "Let me think about it. I'll call you back."

"Boss." The cowboy jerked a thumb in the direction of the horse barn as he called out to Chad. "Someone in there lookin' to buy a horse."

Chad lifted a hand in acknowledgement and veered in that direction. He was dirty, tired, and thirsty. He didn't feel like talking to anyone just now. Besides, he really didn't have any horses he wanted to part with at the moment. He pulled up short in the doorway.

And especially not that one! He glowered at the shadowed figure standing outside of Maybelle's stall. The prospective buyer raised a hand, palm flat, to offer the horse a treat and something in the tentativeness of the woman's movement rang an alarm in his gut. She turned slightly, putting her form in profile to him, and his heart picked up the warning clang.

"Megan?"

His eyes adjusted to the dim light and he saw her chin lift to a proud, stubborn angle.

"Hello, Chad. I heard you're selling off some stock and, um, and thought I'd make an offer for this horse."

Slowly, he closed the distance between them. She seemed as skittish as a new foal.

"Of course, I'd need somewhere to keep it," she rattled on, her words running together, "I mean, I don't have a stock trailer or anything and I don't know the first thing about the care and feeding of a horse, so I was wondering if I bought her, if you'd keep her here, besides she's used to . . ."

"Megan." He cut off the flow of nervous chatter. "What are you doing here?"

"I just told you . . ."

"Bull!"

"But Maybelle . . ."

"I'd *give* you the ever lovin' mare, you know that!"

"Chad . . . I . . ."

"Megan, have you come back to stay?" he demanded, his voice low and rough. "Because if you haven't, I want you off this place now. I can't go through this with you again, woman."

"You . . . you can't?"

He shook his head slowly and took the last two steps that brought him within touching distance of her. His palms, damp with sweat, itched for the feel of her.

He clenched his jaw and closed his hands into fists. Her pupils dilated and her breath seemed to catch in quick little spurts.

Her lips parted and her tongue darted out to make a nervous swipe over them. Someone groaned. Himself, he thought. Someone moved. Both of them perhaps.

It didn't matter. In a heartbeat they were locked in each other's arms, their lips communicating in a way that needed no words. Outside the wide barn door, a cool wind picked up and in the distance, thunder rumbled. Megan drew back just enough to look up into his eyes.

"I want to see the storm from your window," she whispered.

"It won't be anything compared to the one we've been through," he growled. She smiled and his heart turned over.

The next thing he knew, she pulled from his arms and ran for the house, calling over her shoulder, "Last one in has to fix supper!"

"No fair!" he shouted at her retreating figure. Maybelle whickered behind him. "Yeah, girl, she's back," he assured the mare. "Megan is home."

The large jet circled high over verdant pine forests as it waited its turn to touch down at Houston Intercontinental. We're almost home, Megan thought, then reacted with surprise. She didn't think of her parents' house as *home* anymore. Home to her, she realized, was with Chad, wherever that might be. A smile stole across her lips. She'd felt at home with him from the very beginning.

"What are you thinking about?"

His voice held a wary challenge that changed her soft smile to a mischievous grin. "Nothing, why?" she asked innocently.

"Don't give me that. What are you up to now?"

She laughed and kissed his cheek. "I was only thinking how much I love you," she admitted.

"Oh. Well, that's okay then."

She laughed again. "Thank you, exalted master."

"Smart aleck," he snapped, but squeezed her hand affectionately.

"Are we really going house hunting?"

Chad grinned at the reminder of the excuse he'd used to justify the need for Megan to return with him. "Sure."

Her mother had insisted that if they were having a wedding in a few short weeks, Megan needed to stay and help make all the arrangements, but he wasn't about to leave her behind. What he really had in mind was to build them a place a short distance from his parents' house. He had the knoll all picked out, but he wanted her input on choosing floor plans, as well as the interior details. And he didn't want her more than one step away from his arms.

They could take an apartment during the construction, or stay in the old home place. It would be up to her.

Their flight landed and Megan waited impatiently for Chad to claim their luggage. They'd hardly had a moment alone before leaving for Kansas, and she ached for some private time with him. Maybe they could go riding when they got back, or if his parents were still busy at The Depot, they could snuggle in the living room of the ranch house.

Chad found their bags and led her through the crowd, out of the terminal to where the parking lot shuttle buses waited.

"Isn't someone meeting us?"

"No, I had one of the boys bring your car down and leave it yesterday," he explained.

"It's fixed?"

"Seems so."

At the outlying parking area, Chad left her with their suitcases while he retrieved the keys from the lot attendant. "Wait here," he instructed as he kissed her forehead, "I'll get the car and pick you up."

She watched him stride off across the blacktop, then turned toward the parade of traffic passing on the adjoining road.

A horn sounded close behind her and she whirled in panic, only to find herself face to face with her husband-to-be. He grinned at her through the windshield of a bright blue vehicle, but it wasn't her little Escort. Chad sat perched high behind the wheel of a brand-new Bronco. A huge, fluffy red bow decorated the roof and an oversized gift tag dangled down just behind the driver's door.

He climbed out and gently closed her jaw with one fingertip. "Isn't it the right color?" he asked, his smile teasing her.

Her mouth worked a time or two before she could get a sound out. "Ye . . . yes, the color's right, but that's not my car."

He frowned. "No? Are you sure?"

Taking her arm, he led her to the tag and Megan held the large placard by one corner as she read, *To my beloved wife, for safe journeys, from her Truck Stop Cowboy.* She touched trembling fingertips to her lips and breathed, "Oh, Chad."

"You like it?"

Her arms locked around his neck and gave him a smacking kiss on the cheek. "Like it? I love it, but you shouldn't have."

"Hey," he murmured, "none of that. I want you to be safe, I *need* for you to be safe. This journey we're about to start is going to be the best of my life, and I want it to last a long, long time."

She drew back and smiled up at him. "What's your idea of long?"

"Oh, seventy-five years."

"Is that all?"

"Hmmm, I'll look at renewing my option after that, okay?"

"Okay," she whispered, then pulled his head down for a deep, satisfying kiss. Neither of them noticed the passing traffic, the grins of the drivers, or the symphony of blaring horns that filled the afternoon air.

Epilogue

Raised voices drew everyone's attention to a back corner of the diner. Nadine stood against the wall, arms crossed, a snarl on her lips, as a tall, sandy-haired trucker loomed over her.

"You are the most trouble per pound of any woman I've ever met," he fumed.

"Well, you know where the door is, don't let it hit your butt on the way out!"

"And that's another thing!" The lanky man shook a finger in her face. "You're going to clean up that mouth of yours starting right now. No kid of mine is going to spout the trash you talk."

"Who said it's yours?" Nadine gasped. "I don't know where you got *that* da . . ."

"Your mouth, Nadine, I told you to watch your mouth!"

"And you can take a flying leap, Jim Adams!"

"That does it!" Gentleman Jim, Oklahoma truck driver and staunch believer in old-fashioned family values, grabbed Nadine's wrist and pulled her through the kitchen and out the cafe's back door. He spun her to face him. "Now, one more foul word out of that sweet mouth of yours and I'm going to tan your hide!"

Unintimidated, Nadine jerked her hand free. "Sweet?" she mimicked. "There's never been a sweet thing about me and you da . . . darn well know it."

A large hand came up to cup her cheek, the fingers delving into the fine hair at her temple. "Now there you're wrong, darlin'. Those are the sweetest lips I've ever kissed."

Nadine crossed her arms and looked away. Gently he nudged her chin around so she'd meet his eyes.

"I'm crazy about you, don't you know that?"

"So what? It didn't sound like it that last day in Houston," she snarled. "Besides, a lot of men are crazy about me."

"That's another thing I don't want to hear anymore of," he chastised as he smoothed his hand over her hair. "We start from now, just you and me."

Nadine gave a harsh laugh. "Just you and me? What about the little bun in the oven? Does it just disappear?"

Jim's arms came up to gather her close. "No way.

I'm going to take you *and* the little bun home with me. My old Granny will be glad for the company."

"And what if I don't want to go?" Hope was a new concept for someone like Nadine.

"Didn't plan on giving you a choice," came the laconic reply. "Besides, she'll be a great help to you in breaking some of those bad habits of yours."

"Now just a minute, what . . ."

"Habits like cussin', smokin', backtalkin'. There's quite a list, but you're a strong woman, Nadine, you can do it."

"And just why would I want to?" she snapped, but without her usual fervor.

"Because I love you and I want us to make the best possible home for our baby." Jim turned back to the cafe door, once again pulling Nadine along behind him. Half a dozen heads disappeared back into the kitchen as though jerked by strings.

"Come on now, you have packing to do. I'll call ahead so Gran can let the preacher know we're coming to talk to him about a wedding."

"A wedding?" she whispered.

"Yep, and you'll like Gran, wait and see. She can teach you about putting in a vegetable garden, how to can what you grow, how to sew . . ."

Dazed, Nadine trailed behind him protesting weakly, "But . . . but . . ."